Girl Who Chases Ghosts

An Ella Porter Mystery Thriller

Georgia Wagner

Contents

Prologue

The flickering glow of the television screen cast eerie shadows across the living room, dancing on the pale blue wallpaper. Margaret sat alone, her eyes glued to the screen, as the weatherman droned on about an incoming storm. She pulled the woolen blanket tighter around her shoulders, trying to keep the chill at bay.

A sudden gust of wind rattled the window pane, causing her to jump in her seat. The howling Alaskan wind had been relentless all evening, and it was starting to fray her nerves. With a frustrated sigh, she got up from her comfortable armchair and approached the stubborn window.

"Damn latch," she muttered under her breath, her fingers fumbling with the rusty metal. Margaret could feel the icy draft slipping through the cracks like frigid ghosts. Her frustration grew with each futile attempt to close the window.

She gave the latch one last tug before admitting defeat. Glancing back at the television, she paused, frowning. Had she heard a noise from the side of the house? She hesitated, feeling a shiver crawl down her spine that had nothing to do with the cold.

"It's just the wind," she told herself, rubbing her hands together for warmth. But even as she tried to reassure herself, she couldn't shake the growing sense of unease that had taken hold of her.

With a deep breath, Margaret returned to her armchair, tucking herself back under the blanket. She tried to focus on the television, hoping to distract herself from the ominous wind that continued to torment her. It was just another lonely night in Alaska she assured herself as she settled back into her solitary vigil.

And then it happened again. Margaret's focus on the television was disrupted by a sudden noise from the alley behind her house. It was a guttural, animalistic sound that cut through the howling wind, sending a shiver down her spine.

"Get it together, Margaret," she whispered to herself, clenching her wool cover, but her curiosity piqued. She set the blanket aside, pulled on her slippers, and cautiously approached the back door. The old wooden floor creaked beneath her feet, protesting each step she took. Margaret pressed her ear against the door, straining to hear any further noises.

"Is someone out there?" she said, her faint voice shaking in the high winds, her heart pounding in her chest. She considered calling out louder, but fear held her tongue. Instead, she flicked on the outdoor light and peered through the small window, scanning the narrow alley.

There, amidst the shadowy darkness, she spotted the source of the distressing sound: a scrawny stray cat, its fur matted and eyes wild, gnawing at a discarded scrap of food. Relief washed over Margaret as she recognized the harmless creature; however, the eerie feeling lingered.

She tapped on the glass to scare the cat away. The feline turned its yellow gaze on her before darting off into the night. Margaret sighed and retreated back to the living room, leaving the unsettling atmosphere of the alley behind her.

She chided herself as she returned to her armchair.

But she paused again, staring at the television now.

What... the hell...

She blinked, fixated on the image on the screen.

The television now displayed a scene she didn't recognize—an empty room, dimly lit and devoid of furnishings, save for a solitary chair positioned in the center. The camera seemed to be zooming in on the chair ever so slowly, creating an uneasy tension.

She wrinkled her nose, searching for the remote control. But as she fumbled through the folds of her blanket, she couldn't tear her eyes away from the screen. The image grew more ominous with each passing second, and Margaret felt an inexplicable dread creeping into her bones.

Suddenly, the image on the television screen changed. A cacophony of static erupted from the speakers, causing Margaret to jump in her seat. The sound sent shivers down her spine. She gasped aloud, gripping the armrests of her chair tightly.

As the static began to dissipate, an image flickered into view: a handsome man, his face streaked with tears, bound to the very same chair that had occupied the empty room moments ago. Margaret recognized him instantly, her breath catching in her throat.

"Governor Hunt?" she whispered in disbelief, her heart pounding.

"Please... please don't hurt me," the governor sobbed, his voice trembling. "I—I've done everything you asked. Just let me go!"

Margaret's hand flew to her mouth in shock, her eyes glued to the screen. The governor's desperate pleas tore at her heartstrings. Her mind raced, trying to make sense of the chilling scene before her.

"Governor, say it," demanded a cold, disembodied voice from off-screen. The governor hesitated, choking back another sob.

"No," he said. "No, please."

"Say it!" the off-screen voice demanded, louder. A threat was behind those words.

Governor Hunt, who Margaret had seen in more than one political ad on this very screen, whimpered. He opened his mouth. "Tag. You're it, Jameson Porter," he forced out through gritted teeth, his expression a mixture of terror and despair.

The words echoed in Margaret's head as she watched in stunned silence. She couldn't tear her gaze away from the governor's tear-streaked face, nor could she shake the growing sense of dread that enveloped her like a suffocating fog.

"Who's Jameson Porter?" she wondered, her mind racing with potential connections.

"Good," the voice replied, almost pleased. "Now do it."

The governor closed his eyes, resignation etched across his features. With trembling fingers, he raised a gun to his temple...

Margaret stared.

"Please," the governor moaned.

"DO IT OR ELSE!"

Hunt pulled the trigger. The deafening sound of the gunshot reverberated through Margaret's living room, drowning out the relentless Alaskan wind.

"No!" Margaret cried out, her voice strangled by shock and horror.

She stared at the television screen, her mind reeling as she tried to process what she had just witnessed. The governor of Alaska, dead by his own hand on live television. And all because of some mysterious figure named Jameson Porter.

As the television flickered and the image of the governor's lifeless body faded to black, Margaret's scream tore through the silence, echoing off the walls of her living room. Her heart thundered in her chest, adrenaline flooding her veins.

"God... Oh, God," she muttered under her breath, feeling sick to her stomach. She couldn't get the image of the governor's lifeless body out of her mind—the blood splattered on the wall behind him, his eyes wide open and unseeing.

Panic surged within her, urging her into action. Margaret stumbled to her feet and rushed across the room, her legs shaky but determined. She grabbed the phone from its cradle on the hallway table, her fingers fumbling over the buttons as she dialed 911.

"Come on, come on," she whispered, her voice trembling with fear and urgency. The line trilled once, twice, before finally connecting.

"9-1-1, what's your emergency?" a calm, professional voice answered.

"I—I just saw Governor Thompson kill himself on TV!" Margaret blurted out, her words tumbling over each other. "He said something about 'Jameson Porter' and then he shot himself!"

"Ma'am, we've received the call already. Thank you."

And the operator hung up.

She stared at the phone in her hand... The 9-1-1 operator had just hung up on her.

What the hell was going on?

Chapter 1

Ella Porter sat rigidly in the passenger seat of the sleek, black SUV, her eyes fixed on the road ahead. Her breath fogged up the cold window, momentarily obscuring the barren landscape that zipped past them. She stole a glance at the man behind the wheel, Mortimer Graves—a middle-aged British gentleman with a shock of gray hair, his hands steady on the steering wheel as he navigated the desolate stretch of asphalt.

Graves had an air of sophistication about him, from the tailored charcoal suit that hugged his lean frame to the faint scent of sandalwood that clung to him. The quiet intensity in his icy eyes seemed to cut through Ella, making her feel exposed and vulnerable despite the layers of clothing.

"Your father's operation is quite impressive," Graves remarked casually, his voice smooth like honey but tainted with an underlying edge of something darker, sending chills down Ella's spine.

"Mhmm," she replied noncommittally, returning her gaze to the window, determined not to engage further in conversation.

They still hadn't discussed what he'd shown her on the video feed. He hadn't told her where he was taking her either.

She shot him another sidelong glance and felt shivers down her spine. She pictured the horrible images on his phone. The two assassins he'd captured... bound...

She opened her mouth now, ready to demand answers, but then a melodic ringtone filled the cabin, and Graves pulled out his phone. "Excuse me, I have to take this," he said, his tone shifting into one of tenderness, a stark contrast to his previous demeanor. Accepting the call, Graves spoke softly, each word dripping with affection, "Hello, buddy. How was your day?"

As the conversation continued, Ella couldn't help but wonder if this gentler side of Graves was genuine or just another layer of deception. Listening closely, she strained to make out the faint voice on the other end of the line.

She bit her lip, her thoughts racing as they delved deeper into unknown territory.

"Alright, we'll talk later. Love you too." Graves ended the call, his voice returning to its natural timbre. He glanced at Ella, who quickly averted her gaze, trying to mask the suspicion that had been consuming her during the call.

"Family is important," he said simply, as if to explain away the tenderness in his voice. But for Ella, his words only deepened the mystery surrounding this enigmatic man—a serial killer. Yet one who hunted evil men.

Still, Ella's patience was wearing thin. She clenched her fists tightly, her knuckles turning white as she finally demanded, "Where are you taking me, Graves? Enough with the secrecy."

Graves glanced at her briefly, his gray eyes betraying no emotion. "You'll see soon enough," he said curtly, focusing back on the road.

Frustration bubbled up inside her, but she knew pressing him further would be fruitless. Ella took a deep breath and stared out the window, watching the landscape blur past them. Trees lined both sides of the highway, their branches swaying in the wind like skeletal fingers reaching for something just out of grasp.

"Are they still alive?" Ella said suddenly. "Those men you captured?"

"You mean the men who tried to kill you?"

"Yes."

A long pause stretched between them, giving space for Ella's mind to churn with speculation on the things her murderous ally might have done to his captives.

"Here," Graves said suddenly, breaking Ella from her thoughts. He pulled a sleek smartphone from his pocket and tapped the screen a few times before showing it to her.

The image displayed on the screen made her heart skip a beat. Two identical, Italian-looking men were tied up in what appeared to be a dimly lit basement. They were naked, their muscular bodies marred by cuts and bruises. Their fierce eyes glared into the camera, a mix of fury and fear swirling within them. Ella remembered those faces all too well.

"Where do you... have them?" Ella stammered, staring at the screen.

"Nearby. I thought you might want to have a little chat with them," Graves replied, his voice dripping with satisfaction.

Ella's heart hammered in her chest as she stared at the image of the captured assassins on Graves' phone. The cold, dimly-lit, concrete space where they were held captive sent a chill down her spine. Her mind raced with questions.

Graves pocketed his phone and glanced over at her, his gray eyes unreadable. "I don't think it would be wise for me to divulge that information just yet, Agent Porter. Trust is a delicate thing, after all."

"Trust? You're showing me two men who tried to kill me, tied up and beaten..."

"Exactly. Clearly, I'm on your side, yes?"

He gave her a wink and allowed himself a small, knowing smile. "Ah, but I didn't harm them," Graves replied calmly, his hands steady on the wheel as he navigated the winding road. "They came to me like that. I simply... secured them, for your benefit."

Ella's jaw clenched, her frustration mounting. She needed answers, not riddles. "Take me to them. Now." She stared fiercely at Graves, daring him to defy her.

He let out a soft chuckle, shaking his head slightly. "All in good time, Agent Porter. All in good time." He accelerated around a tight bend, sending gravel spraying from under the SUV's tires. "Rest assured, I will take you to them. But first, we need to discuss our next steps."

"Fine," Ella said cagily, her mind working furiously to piece together what Graves' true intentions might be. She couldn't shake the feeling that there was more going on than met the eye, and she needed to tread carefully. For now, she'd play his game—but she vowed not to let her guard down for a second.

"Once I see them," she added, her voice firm and resolute, "we can talk about whatever you want. But not until then."

"Very well, Agent Porter," Graves agreed, his tone placid and controlled. "But remember, trust is a two-way street. You'll have to show me that you can trust me as well."

Ella's grip tightened on the door handle, her knuckles turning white. Trust would be hard to come by in this situation, but if it meant getting closer to the truth, she was willing to take the risk.

A heavy silence hung in the air as the SUV sped down the winding road. Dark clouds rolled in overhead, casting an ominous shadow over the desolate landscape. They were driving away from Nome—she thought she knew this route. The wind picked up, whipping through the gnarled branches of the trees that lined the road, their leaves rustling in protest.

"Looks like a storm's brewing," Graves commented, his eyes flicking to the rearview mirror. "Perfect timing, don't you think?"

"Is that supposed to mean something?"

"Only that it adds a touch of drama to our little adventure," he replied, a faint smirk playing on his lips.

"Ah, there. See? I'm taking you to home turf. Another gesture of goodwill."

And now Ella realized why she recognized the terrain. Ahead, she spotted a road buttressed by piles of mud and tailings, the ground gouged with heavy wheel imprints.

As they approached her father's inland mining operation, the oppressive atmosphere intensified. Lightning flashed in the distance, illuminating the hulking machinery and dilapidated buildings that loomed ahead.

Ella's heart skipped as she stared out the window, her mind whirling with uncertainty.

All of this started and ended with the Collective.

A secret society of murderers. A sordid group of twisted minds and killers who were involved in a game of death. Ella didn't know much about them, except that her father had information on them and that the Collective was funded by a man known only as the Architect, said to be a sociopathic billionaire who delighted in the chaos he caused.

This had all started years ago she supposed. Ella remembered releasing Graves from custody. He'd helped put a child predator in the ground. Someone the FBI hadn't been able to catch. And now... she realized she was paying for flouting the rules. This was her recompense.

The SUV slowed to a stop before a rusted gate, barricading the entrance to one of the abandoned warehouses. Graves put the car in park and stepped out, leaving Ella alone with her thoughts. She watched him unchain the gate, his movements methodical and precise, as if he'd done this countless times before.

Her hands clenched into fists on her lap, her nails digging into her palms. Despite the storm outside, a bead of sweat trickled down her temple. She couldn't shake the nagging feeling that she was walking into a trap, but there was no turning back now.

"Chin up, Eleanor," Graves called as he returned to the car to drive through the now open gate. "We're almost there."

Ella hesitated for a moment, then took a deep breath, steeling herself for whatever lay ahead.

Ella's heart thundered in her chest, the sound of rain pelting against the car windows only heightening her growing unease. She couldn't help but imagine the worst as she stared out into the gloom, the storm swallowing the rugged landscape as they continued toward the old warehouse looming large on the other side of the gate. The heavy air weighed on her, mirroring the gravity of the situation.

"Here we are, Agent Porter," Graves announced, his tone infuriatingly calm despite the tension that coiled within her. He steered the SUV through a muddy parking lot, the wind howling around them like a malevolent spirit. It screamed a warning she couldn't ignore, yet she was powerless to act upon it.

The SUV pulled up in front of the decrepit warehouse, its weathered façade a testament to years of neglect. As they climbed out into the storm, the biting wind tore through Ella's clothes, chilling her to the bone. But it wasn't just the cold that made her shiver—something about the place felt wrong, as if all the shadowed gloom in the world had been hidden away here.

"Inside," Graves said curtly, raising his hand to shield his eyes from the rain as he unlocked the warehouse door. The rusty hinges groaned in protest as he pushed it open, revealing a gaping maw of darkness beyond.

"Graves," Ella began, her ever-present poker face slipping to reveal a frown. She was always good at keeping her emotions in check. Or, as her boyfriend accused her, of keeping them *concealed*. But now, she allowed her displeasure to crease her pretty, pale features. Her blue eyes narrowed, her upturned nose tilted along with her sharp chin as she peered at the middle-aged British killer. "I need to know what's going on. How did you capture them?:

"Trust me, Eleanor," he said, turning to look at her, his gray eyes piercing through the rain. "You want answers? They're inside. Now, are you coming or not?"

With a final glance at the ominous building before them, Ella took a deep breath and followed Graves into the shadows, praying she'd made the right choice.

The darkness inside the warehouse seemed to swallow them whole as Ella and Graves stepped across the threshold. Her eyes took a moment to adjust, but soon enough she could make out the silhouettes of objects scattered throughout the cavernous space. The air was damp and moldy, adding to the unsettling atmosphere. She could detect the strong odor of machine oil and grease.

"Stay close," Graves whispered, his voice barely audible above the howling wind that now echoed through the vast emptiness.

As they ventured further in, Ella's heart thumped in her chest, each beat a plea for answers. She glanced at Graves, searching for any hint of trepidation on his face, but she found none. The man remained an enigma, his stoic expression betraying little about what lay ahead. He even paused to adjust his sleeves, as if a crease in the charcoal fabric bothered him.

Suddenly, the beam of a flashlight cut through the darkness, casting sinister shadows on the walls.

Ella paused. She could hear breathing. Faint puffs of air, coming from the dark of the warehouse.

Her eyes strained in the darkness, trying to pick out the source of the unnerving noises.

Graves directed the light towards the far end of the warehouse, where two men were bound to chairs, their faces contorted in a mixture of rage and fear. The identical twins bore the unmistakable features of Italian descent—dark hair, olive skin, and sharp, angular features. But now those features were twisted with fury.

"Here they are," Graves said coldly, keeping his distance as he shone the flashlight on the captives. "The men who tried to kill you."

Ella stared at the bound assassins, her stomach churning as she recalled the near-death experience. Brenner lying on the floor of his apartment, fire raging around them.

The assassins glared back at her, venom in their eyes as if they could still carry out their mission even in this state. A storm of questions raged within her, threatening to spill forth in a torrent of anger and confusion.

She glanced at Graves, but he said nothing, just waiting patiently.

She then summoned her inner resolve, suppressed any fear, and took a step forward, striding towards the two killers.

Chapter 2

Ella's eyes burned with determination as she stared down the two assassins, their wrists bound and seated on cold metal and wood chairs. The room was dimly lit, casting eerie shadows onto the concrete walls. Her skin prickled with a thin glaze of sweat under her winter jacket, knowing that the information she sought could lead her closer to the Architect.

"Tell me about the man who sent you," Ella demanded, her voice steady despite the adrenaline coursing through her veins.

The assassins exchanged looks, their eyes filled with mockery. Neither of them said anything

"Fine," she said, narrowing her eyes. "Let's try this again. What is your connection to the Architect?"

Again, neither of them spoke.

They were her only link to the Architect, and she couldn't afford to lose that link. She focused on their expressions and body language, trying to find a crack in their armor.

"From the way you obey the Architect, I can tell you're afraid of him," Ella said, her voice low and measured. "But I can guarantee you'll be more afraid of my friend here if you don't start cooperating."

"Is that a threat?" the first assassin asked, speaking for the first time, his eyes hooded, his face bruised and scratched.

"Call it whatever you want," Ella replied, her eyes locked onto his. "But I'm not the one you should fear. Though... guessing by your current state of dress..." She glanced at Graves who smirked, "I'm guessing you're already acquainted with my friend."

"We're friends now, hmm?" Graves said. "Delightful."

The two assassins shared another glance, their eyes communicating, though their lips remained motionless. Ella knew she had hit a nerve, but she needed to dig deeper.

"Listen," she continued, her voice cold as ice. "You may think you're untouchable because you work for the Architect, but trust me, there are worse fates than crossing him. Now, you're going to tell me everything you know, or I'll make sure you wish you had."

It was a strong-arm tactic and not one she normally favored. But she was already well past her comfort zone.

She'd followed a serial killer to her father's mining operation in order to illegally detain and question two men who certainly looked as if they'd been tortured, or at least roughed up a bit.

As the weight of her words settled over the room, the assassins' confidence began to crumble, replaced by renewed flickers of fear. Though perhaps this had to do with the way Graves had bent slowly to pick a rusted chain off the ground. He was playing with it, allowing the ominous clink of metal to draw the attention of the bound men.

"Well, boys?" said Mortimer quietly. "Are we going to start chatting, or do we have to separate you two?"

The way he said it, so casually, as if reprimanding some misbehaving child, sent shivers down Ella's back. One of the men spat at Graves.

It was like a starter pistol for a race. The middle-aged man bounded across the room in a blur like someone youthful.

Mortimer's eyes gleamed with determination as he grabbed the bound assailant roughly by the arm and hauled him to his feet. The assassin who'd spat struggled against Mortimer's grip, but it was futile—he was in no state to put up much of a fight.

"Wait!" cried the second assassin, panic creeping into his voice.

For a moment, Ella feared Mortimer would kill the man.

But he dragged him towards the door, pulling him by his bound hands.

The man let out guttural sounds of exertion as he tried to scramble back.

But it was to no avail. Graves pulled open the door and allowed a gust of icy wind to come through.

And then, he flung the unclothed man out into the snow, before following him out.

As the door slammed shut behind Mortimer and the first assassin, the second killer's previous smugness was replaced by genuine agitation. His eyes darted around the room, searching for a way to escape or some sort of leverage to use against Ella. But he found none, only the steely determination in her eyes as she continued her line of questioning.

"Start talking," she demanded, her heart pounding with adrenaline. "And we'll let him back in."

Even as she said it, she felt a surge of guilt. She couldn't allow Mortimer to freeze the other killer to death. She glanced surreptitiously at her phone. She'd give it a minute. No longer. Even a minute could cause damage, but it wouldn't kill him. Not this close to a heated structure.

Part of her wanted to turn, to call out to Graves to bring the man back in.

But in for a penny, in for a pound.

The moment Ella had gotten into the car with Graves, she'd known what she'd been doing.

At least... she thought she did.

Now, she wasn't so sure.

She couldn't hear any sound from the other side of the door. She hoped this meant Graves was just waiting patiently.

A little bit of cold...

That's all it was if she could get this second man to talk.

"The longer we wait, the worse it is for him," she said hurriedly. There was a note of urgency in her voice that wasn't feigned. "Neither of us want that."

"Let him back in!" snarled the second man.

"I'd like to. I really would. But believe it or not, that man doesn't work for me. So why don't you get us *both* what we want? Hmm? Tell me who sent you."

"Let him back in!"

"Depends on what you have to say," Ella replied, her voice steady despite the tension that gripped her.

As the snow continued to fall outside, visible through the glass above the door, Ella pressed on, "This can all be over soon, sir. He's out th ere... Hypothermia sets in quick in Alaska. You don't look like you're from around here..."

But the man just snarled, "If I tell you shit, he'll do worse to us."

Ella shrugged. "He? Is that the Architect?"

"Go to hell."

"Too cold for that."

The door creaked open, and a gust of chilly air rushed in as Graves entered the room. Ella glanced over at him, her eyes narrowing as he approached. In his hand, he held up a key, dangling it between his thumb and forefinger like a lifeline. She studied him for a moment, noting the glint in his eyes and the bead of sweat that traced a path down the side of his forehead from his momentary exertion. She spotted no sign of the second killer. But then her eyes moved to the car, the lights on... which meant the heat was on. A shape was visible in the back seat. The man was in the heated car.

Ella felt a flicker of relief. But the brother didn't know this.

Ella's gaze flicked between the car key—which Mortimer clearly displayed for her benefit—and the second assassin, who was growing increasingly agitated.

The room fell silent, tension hanging heavy in the air like a suffocating fog. As the seconds ticked by, Grave's grip tightened on the key, his determination unwavering.

Ella studied the second assassin, the man's eyes darting between her and Graves. The dim light cast eerie shadows across his face, making him look even more sinister. She leaned in, catching a whiff of sweat mixed with fear.

"Alright," the assassin finally muttered, his voice barely above a whisper. "I know the Architect. But I don't know much else."

"Tell me what you do know," Ella demanded, her pulse quickening.

"Let my brother back in! Now!"

"Tell me what you know!" she retorted, bolstered by the knowledge that the second man was in a heated vehicle.

The assassin licked his dry lips, hesitating for just a moment before he continued. "There's something big coming—something that'll change everything. But that's all I can tell you."

"Change everything?" Ella echoed. "What does that mean?"

"I don't know!" the assassin snapped, frustration creeping into his voice.

His calm demeanor seemed to crack, but as Ella scrutinized him, she couldn't shake the nagging feeling that something wasn't quite right. She knew these types of people, and they rarely showed their true emotions. In the back of her mind, she wondered if it was all just an act.

"Try harder," she growled, her patience wearing thin. "You must know something."

"Really, I don't!" the assassin insisted, his voice raising an octave. He looked genuinely desperate now, but Ella couldn't afford to let her guard down. She needed to push him further, to break through whatever barrier was keeping him from revealing the truth.

"Think!" Ella shouted, her voice echoing off the cold concrete walls. She could feel her blood boiling beneath her skin, frustration and anger threatening to consume her. She needed answers, and she needed them now. The image of Brenner surrounded by fire was seared in her mind. They'd nearly taken him from her... Nearly killed the man she loved.

The assassin's eyes flicked to the side for just a moment, and Ella's gut clenched. A bead of sweat trickled down his temple as he continued to feign ignorance, shaking his head, pleading.

He was agitated, moving back and forth, straining against his bonds.

Graves watched closely, eyes narrowed.

And it was in that moment Ella hesitated.

The assassin was moving *too* much. As if attempting to shield her view of...

His hands.

She realized now she couldn't see his hands bound behind him.

"Wait a second," she said, her eyes narrowing. She had been so focused on getting information from him that she hadn't noticed the subtle shift in his posture.

Nor the frayed fragments of rope scattered across the ground behind him from where he'd worried through the rope. A flash of metal in his right hand. A screw? A knife?

The assassin didn't give her a chance to figure it out. he was already moving, lunging at her with a feral scream.

Ella barely had time to react, her body moving on instinct alone. The sharp screw glinted in the assassin's hand as he lunged at Ella, targeting her jugular.

With the reflexes of a seasoned agent, Ella raised her arm to intercept the screw. The cold metal bit into her flesh, sending a searing pain up her arm. But her sacrifice paid off, stopping the slicing blow.

She shoved off him, stumbling back and keeping her distance.

He stared at them, eyes wide, panic flaring through his gaze.

"Drop it," Graves said quietly.

Ella glanced back and realized the serial killer had a gun in hand and was pointing it directly at the assassin's chest.

"You think you know who you're playing with?" the assassin snarled. "Hmm? My brother... he's dead now. Isn't he?"

"I said drop it," Graves retorted.

"Yeah... yeah..." Ella watched as if in slow motion as the assassin's hand tensed on the screw. His eyes widened as if in some madness, and then he moved.

"No!" she yelled. But too late.

He reached up, gouging the screw into his jugular, and dragging it across his neck.

"Damn you!" he choked out, blood bubbling from the wound as he stumbled backward.

She stared as he collapsed, choking on his own blood. And then she burst forward.

"Don't!" Graves yelled. He caught her wrist, holding her back.

"He's dying!" she yelled.

But he held on. "He's armed. He'll slice you if you get near."

"Graves, let me go, he's—"

"There's nothing you can do to help him," Graves said simply.

Ella yanked her arm away, once more moving to help the bleeding suspect.

But then there were two loud gunshots.

She froze.

The man went still, lying in a pool of blood.

She looked back at Graves, who held his weapon up. He nodded at the dead man and then holstered his gun.

"Couldn't be helped," he said with a sniff. "Pity." He dabbed at his lips with the edge of his sleeve as if he'd just finished a five-course meal. Then he turned, moving back towards the door. "The other one is in the car," he said as if nothing had just happened.

Ella turned back to see two blossoms of red spreading across the assassin's bare chest.

Dead.

His throat slit, blood on his chest... Dead.

All of it in her father's inland mining outfit. Was that an intentional move on Graves' part too?

She gripped her phone tightly in her hand, brow sweaty, breath coming in puffs.

She never should've trusted Graves.

Now she had no information, and she was an accessory to murder.

As these troubled thoughts plagued her, causing her stomach to tie in knots, Ella's phone vibrated, the relentless buzzing refusing to be ignored. She fumbled with her gloves, struggling to grip the device. The screen was flooded with missed calls and urgent text messages.

She swiped across the screen, her breath frosting in the frigid air as she pressed the phone to her ear.

"Chief Baker?" she said.

"Governor Hunt," the voice on the other end said, panicked and out of breath. "He just killed himself. On live TV."

She blinked.

"Sorry... what did you just say?"

"Dammit, Ella. All hands on. Come in. *Now*!" And then her brother-in-law, the Nome Chief of Police, hung up.

Chapter 3

Ella shivered, gripping the wheel of the dirt truck as she maneuvered up the cramped streets of Nome.

She'd refused to get in a car with Graves. She couldn't. Not after he'd shot the man...

Then again, the man had already been bleeding out.

She shook her head. In her horror at the way things had ended, Ella hadn't considered the *second* assassin.

Now she didn't know where he was. With Graves... somewhere. She shivered, glancing in her rearview mirror on instinct alone, and shaking her head in frustration.

Brenner was still asleep back in the motel room. Ella adjusted her golden bangs from her blue eyes, glancing through the windshield now as wind howled around her.

She sped into the parking lot of the police precinct, a plain-faced structure which faced the Bering Sea. The air smelled of saline and moisture.

She received more than one odd glance as she veered into the parking lot, hopped a curb in the old, rusted dirt truck from her father's mining site, and then dropped out onto the asphalt.

Ella pushed open the heavy glass door of the police precinct, a gust of frigid Alaskan air nipping at her heels. The fluorescent lights overhead buzzed and flickered, casting stark shadows across the worn linoleum floor. A uniformed officer glanced up from his paperwork as she approached, his eyes scanning her face before nodding in recognition.

"Agent Porter," he said, extending a hand to shake. "Chief Baker's expecting you. His office is down the hall, last door on the left."

"Thank you," Ella replied curtly, her grip firm in the handshake. She could feel a growing knot of anxiety in her stomach, fueled by the phone call she'd received. Baker had seemed scared.

As she made her way deeper into the precinct, her thoughts were interrupted by the familiar click of high heels echoing through the corridor.

"Where do you think you're going?" Priscilla Porter demanded, her arms crossed and brows furrowed. Ella's twin sister had an uncanny ability to appear when least expected, like a specter from the past that refused to fade away.

"Cilla, this is official business. Not now." Ella sighed, attempting to keep her calm. Their relationship had always been strained, the weight of childhood rivalry never quite lifted.

"Considering our father's name was mentioned before the governor killed himself, I'd say it's my business too." Priscilla's voice trembled with barely contained fear, her fingers digging into her forearms. Her blonde hair was tied back in a ponytail, and her arms were crossed as if she were trying to twist a knot around her torso.

Ella paused, studying her sister's face for any sign of deception. But all she found was genuine fright.

"Dad's name was brought up?"

"Yeah. Where have you been?" snapped Cilla.

"Just..." Ella trailed off, trying not to picture the corpse now lying on the warehouse floor.

She shook her head. "Just—wait... what about Dad?"

Priscilla frowned, standing in the hall in front of her husband's office door. Behind her, Ella spotted black lettering on the door which simply read *Chief M. Baker*. "What about Dad?" Ella insisted more urgently.

"Hunt mentioned his name before shooting himself. Said Dad was next."

"Where is he now?"

"Hiding. Protected. Don't you worry."

Ella stared at her twin, the two of them mirroring each other's features. "Shit, really? You think I'd hurt him?"

"I didn't say that... But now that you mention it, it's not like you and Dad were ever particularly fond of each other, were you?"

Cilla was breathing heavily now, her face flushed and tinged with red.

"So Dad's safe?"

"For now."

"Alright, whatever. I'm speaking with Baker."

"He's *my* husband!" Cilla turned promptly, grabbed the door handle and flung it open. "Just stay out of my way."

"Deal," Ella replied, her expression unreadable.

As they walked side by side, Ella couldn't help but dwell on their tumultuous history. Cilla had seen herself as the responsible one, the rock that held their family together. She currently ran their father's off-shore mining business and was starting to make inroads into the inland operation as well.

Ella, on the other hand, had joined the feds.

"Just don't get in the way," Ella warned as they pushed through Baker's door. "And don't make things worse."

"Wouldn't dream of it," Priscilla said, her voice dripping with sarcasm. But beneath the biting tone, Ella could sense her sister's fear.

The moment Ella and Priscilla stepped into the office, they were engulfed by a cacophony of voices and activity. Officers rushed past them, their faces etched with worry and determination. Overhead, multiple screens displayed news reports of Governor Hunt's suicide, each relaying the same harrowing images and tragic details. The office was much larger than Ella had anticipated—more like a conference room than anything.

Ella scanned the room, her gaze landing on a tall man with dark hair and a chiseled jaw who was busy barking orders at his subordinates.

"Baker!" Ella called out, catching the man's attention. He strode towards them, his expression grim.

"Ella, glad you're here," he said, his voice tense. "And, er, Cilla—hey, honey."

"Don't hey me. What's going on, Mattie?"

Baker shifted uncomfortably, leaning one hand against a large, oak desk at his side. He sidestepped a projector that was illuminating a whiteboard and leaned towards them, speaking quietly as he did. "Not good. The death was confirmed a few minutes ago. It was Hunt."

"What happened? I need every detail."

"Follow me." Chief Baker led them to a small, cluttered desk—his own, judging by the nameplate on the surface. He stood by his chair, though, and didn't sit. He then pointed at a video streaming on his computer. It looped. Again and again...

Each image showing the governor raising a weapon and pulling the trigger.

"Shit," Ella said, wincing and glancing away after the second replay.

Baker didn't seem to notice. "Governor Hunt committed suicide at 8:15 PM today," he began, pausing the video at the exact moment when the governor pulled the trigger. "There were at least twenty witnesses who saw it on television, including a local woman named

Margaret Whittaker, a key eyewitness. According to her statement, her television channel was hijacked by the broadcast."

Ella stared at the paused image on the screen, trying to glean any additional details.

"Chief, has anyone checked the governor's home?" Ella asked. "Maybe there's something there that could shed light on this."

"Good idea," Chief Baker agreed. "You'll have access to the home. Just keep me informed of any developments."

"Hang on... where was this video taken?"

"That's just it. We don't know."

Ella stared. "So... do we have the body?"

"No. Not yet. But the governor went missing six hours ago, and facial recognition confirmed it's him." A finger pointed towards the screen.

"Enough about that old bag of bribes," snapped Cilla, glaring over the desk at her husband. "What about *Dad*? Are you going to send more uniforms over, Mattie?"

"I've sent everyone I can spare," Chief Baker said to his wife, giving her an imploring look.

But she didn't seem interested in reciprocating. Her foot was tapping urgently against the floor, and her arms had crossed again.

"He's not safe," Cilla said.

"Sounds like he's much safer than the governor," Ella pointed out. She'd thought the comment was innocuous enough, but her sister rounded on her, eyes flashing.

"You never did like him," she snapped. "You don't care if he's next. In fact, I bet you'd welcome it!"

Ella blinked at the sudden acerbic diatribe.

She took a slow, steadying breath. But Cilla, who was used to Ella's self-calming techniques, cut in before Ella could reply.

"Yeah... I wouldn't be surprised if she was involved in this, Mattie."

Baker was massaging the bridge of his nose, clearly used to his wife when she got into this sort of state. He was just shaking his head, but he was also too intimidated by Cilla to directly correct her. Instead, he said, in a wheedling tone, "We're pulling everyone we can. Ella has federal resources. We need her on this, dear."

Cilla's arms were still crossed.

"Fine," she said. "But you'd better keep dad safe—or there'll be hell to pay."

Baker nodded, his expression as serious as he could make it.

"Of course, sweetie." He glanced over where a new projection was sent to the whiteboard, showing the make and model of the gun used in the video.

Within minutes, the room was a flurry of activity as everyone reacted to this new, albeit small, piece of evidence.

"Let's go," Cilla said, a determined look on her face.

Ella glanced over. "Excuse me?"

"I said let's *go*!" snapped Cilla. "Do I have to do your job for you?"

"Where exactly are we going?" Ella said slowly.

Cilla pointed at the whiteboard. "She's local. The witness who called it in... Margaret Whittaker. Were you even paying attention?"

"Yes. What about her?"

"We're going to speak with her," Cilla snapped.

"I... I don't think I can bring you with me. You're not law enforcement."

Cilla hesitated, scowled, then rounded on her husband. "Deputize me!" she demanded.

Baker blinked.

"Now," Cilla said. It wasn't a request.

Baker sighed, shrugging once. He didn't even try to dissuade her. Instead, he muttered quickly under his breath, "Fine. You got it."

He reached into his pocket, produced a badge, and handed it to Cilla.

She snatched it without ceremony and spun around, nodding towards the exit.

"Let's go speak to this witness," she said.

Ella followed her sister out, taking one last look at the chilling image of Governor Hunt before leaving. Throughout the whole conversation, she had remained calm, but deep down she felt a sense of dread.

Everything was unraveling; she just needed to find the smallest thread.

She couldn't shake the feeling that they were in for a long night.

Chapter 4

The weather was chilly, but it was nothing compared to the interior of the vehicle. Neither of them had spoken for the last twenty minutes as they sped across town in the police cruiser Cilla had essentially commandeered.

Her sister was the Princess of Nome, and so she was accustomed to getting her way, either by dint of her family name or by force of will.

Now, Ella was shifting uncomfortably in the front seat, frowning.

Priscilla, who hadn't said a word since they'd entered the car, gripped the steering wheel tightly. She seemed to resent her sister's presence, and as if in response to Ella's gaze, Cilla floored the accelerator, the car's engine roaring as it sped down the winding Alaskan roads. Snowflakes swirled around them, illuminated by the headlights like a furious dance of ghosts. The wipers worked overtime, trying to keep up with the relentless snowfall.

"Slow down, Cilla!" Ella exclaimed, gripping the door handle. "We won't be able to help anyone if we crash!"

In response, Cilla just went faster. The two of them never could find a compromise, and now Ella was locked in a speeding bullet, trapped with her childhood tormentor.

A daredevil herself, Ella loved tearing across open country on snow-mobiles or dirt bikes. She'd been skydiving and base jumping, and the life-or-death thrill of those sports had appealed to her ever since she'd left Nome as a younger woman. But there was risk-taking and there was recklessness, and her sister's brand of speed definitely fell in the latter category.

Ella gripped the door handle, refusing to speak again lest her sister see it as an invitation to go full *jet mode*.

Finally, the car screeched to a stop in front of a modest home on the edge of town. Crammed between the flurry of the snowstorm, the only light visible was the flicker from a television inside the house.

The storm continued to swirl about them, edging in on the approaching hour of midnight as the sisters pulled up to Margaret's house, a quaint wooden structure nestled deep on the coast of Nome. The snow lay thick on the ground, casting an eerie silence over the scene, broken only by the distant howl of a wolf. Ella's breath fogged up the car window as she peered at the dark house.

"Looks cozy," Priscilla commented, her hands shaking as she turned off the ignition.

"Let's just hope Margaret can help us," Ella replied, her own voice betraying a mix of determination and anxiety. The cold bit at Ella's cheeks, but she barely noticed, her mind focused solely on the task at hand.

Ella and Cilla stumbled away from the car, their faces stinging from the cold. They trudged up to the door. Ella knocked firmly.

In the glass of the sea-facing window, Ella glimpsed the expanse of the gray waters. The Bering Sea stretched out behind them, its slate gray waters mirroring the overcast sky above.

"Looks like we're the only ones here," Priscilla remarked, her eyes scanning the property for any signs of life as she shifted side to side on the porch. She hadn't worn a proper jacket but was too prideful to show just how cold she was as she moved about with antsy motions for warmth.

Ella stepped back, taking in the exterior of the house with an investigator's careful attention. The wood siding was weathered but well-maintained, a testament to Margaret's diligence despite living alone. A small garden bordered the front walkway, the vibrant flowers and lush greenery providing a stark contrast to the barren sea beyond. On closer inspection, though, Ella realized the flowers were plastic. Despite its quaint charm, however, the place appeared deserted. The lights were off, casting the windows in darkness, and the driveway was empty save for their own vehicle. Only the glow of a television illuminated the space inside.

"Doesn't look promising, does it?" Ella muttered, her breath fogging in the chilly air as she tightened her scarf around her neck. She couldn't shake the sinking feeling that had settled in her stomach.

"She's supposed to be here," Cilla said, scowling.

"Maybe she fell asleep," Ella offered. Her fingers drummed anxiously against the door again, her mind racing with all the potential scenarios that could have unfolded before their arrival.

No response.

No sounds.

Ella felt her heart quicken.

"Margaret?" Ella called out tentatively, knocking on the weathered wood a bit harder. There was no response, and a shiver ran down her spine.

But as they stood there, the house seeming to loom larger and more ominously in the fading light, Ella couldn't help but fear the worst.

Ella's hand hovered above the door handle, her breath fogging up in the cold air as she hesitated. Priscilla's gaze met hers, a silent question passing between them: should they enter?

"Margaret?" Ella called out again, louder this time, hoping for some sign of life within the darkened house. But the only response was the distant cry of a seagull, mocking their uncertainty.

"Maybe she didn't hear us," Priscilla suggested, her voice tinged with worry. "Or maybe she's just not here."

"Only one way to find out," Ella replied, steeling herself as she turned the handle. To her surprise, the door swung open easily, revealing a dimly lit hallway.

"Stay close," she whispered, drawing her sidearm and gesturing for Priscilla to follow suit. The pair stepped cautiously inside, their senses on high alert as they scanned the surroundings for any signs of danger.

Cilla, however, didn't step behind her sister. Instead, she stepped alongside, pulling a weapon from inside her waistband.

A fifty caliber, hand cannon. A Desert Eagle if Ella wasn't mistaken.

"Holy shit, Cilla... What's that?"

"Protection. Now shut up. Something doesn't feel right."

They moved further into the house. The air was heavy with an unidentifiable scent—something stale, yet sharp enough to make her eyes water.

"Did you smell that?" she asked Priscilla, who nodded grimly.

"Like something rotten," her sister replied, her own eyes watering as well. "But I don't see anything obviously off."

"Neither do I," Ella agreed, her eyes darting from corner to corner as they continued their search.

Priscilla's grip tightened around her oversized weapon, her knuckles turning white.

As Ella and Priscilla ventured further into the dimly lit house, they found themselves in what appeared to be a living room. A thick layer of dust covered everything, from the outdated furniture to the cobwebs that hung like eerie tapestries from the ceiling. The only light source was the moonlight filtering through the cracked windows, casting distorted shadows across the floor.

"Margaret?" Ella called out, her voice cracking under the weight of the tense atmosphere.

"Over here," Priscilla whispered, her attention drawn to a stack of old newspapers piled high on a coffee table. She picked up the one on top, revealing a headline that read: "Goat wins blue ribbon prize, state fair."

"Look at this," she said, handing the paper to Ella with trembling hands. "This place is a mess."

"Not nearly as nice inside as out," Ella agreed.

Ella furrowed her brow as she scanned the article. "This is from two years ago..."

"Is that significant?"

"I don't know."

They continued their investigation, entering a small kitchen where dirty dishes were piled high in the sink, and moldy food sat forgotten on the countertops. The smell was unbearable, but they pressed on, checking every nook and cranny for any sign of Margaret or clues to her whereabouts.

"Anything?" Ella asked as she rummaged through the cabinets, finding nothing but expired canned goods and mouse droppings.

"Nothing," Priscilla sighed, wiping her hands on her pants after checking beneath the sink. "Let's move on."

"God, what happened here?" Ella muttered, her mind racing with possible scenarios. "Where are you, Margaret? We did call ahead, right?"

"Yeah. She was here," Cilla said. "Right here... this is the address."

They moved upstairs, the wooden steps creaking beneath their feet. The second floor was just as unsettling as the first, with closed doors lining a narrow hallway, each one seemingly hiding secrets behind them.

"Okay, we'll split up," Ella instructed, trying to push away the knot of fear in her stomach. "You take the first two doors; I'll take the last two."

"Got it," Priscilla nodded, her face pale but determined.

The first room Ella entered was a guest bedroom, its bed made immaculately, as if waiting for a visitor who would never come. She pulled open each drawer, finding only neatly folded linens and empty hangers in the closet.

"Nothing in here!" she called out, growing more frustrated with each passing second. She moved on to the next room, which appeared to be Margaret's personal study. There were books scattered across the floor, their covers torn and pages ripped out. Ella knelt down, picking up one that had been left open—a biography about Amelia Earhart.

"Priscilla!" Ella shouted, her voice echoing through the house. "I'm calling this in. We need to get Margaret's phone records."

"Agreed," Priscilla replied, emerging from another room, her eyes narrowed as if the absence of their star witness was a personal insult.

Ella pulled out her cell phone and dialed the station. As she waited for someone to pick up, she glanced around the study, noting the disarray and the sense of urgency that seemed to linger in the air. The call connected, and she quickly explained the situation to the dispatcher.

"Get me Margaret's phone records as soon as you can. Something's not right here," Ella insisted.

Within minutes, the dispatcher sent over the phone records. Ella scrolled through them, her fingers trembling slightly as she searched for any recent activity.

"Look at this," she said, showing the screen to Priscilla. "An unknown number called Margaret's house twenty minutes before we arrived. That's got to be related."

"Someone scared her off," Priscilla whispered, her eyes scanning the room once more. "She left in a hurry. Just look at this place."

Ella nodded, taking in the disheveled state of the room. Papers were strewn about, books ripped apart as if Margaret had been desperately searching for something—or trying to hide it.

"Leaving everything behind like this..." Ella muttered, her heart pounding in her chest. "She must have been terrified."

"Then we have to find her," Priscilla said firmly. "Who would've called her?"

Ella hesitated, thinking about what she knew... The governor was dead. Who'd done it? The two assassins in Nome... one of them was dead. Graves was at large with the other.

Ella looked into Priscilla's determined eyes and felt a surge of adrenaline course through her veins. They were going to find Margaret, no matter what it took.

"Let's go," Ella said, grabbing her coat from a nearby chair. "We're chasing ghosts now, but maybe we can catch up to whatever scared her away."

As they hurried down the stairs, the weight of the mystery seemed to settle upon Ella's shoulders. She knew that time was running out, and with each passing moment, Margaret's safety grew more uncertain.

Chapter 5

They reached the first floor, moving fast. "APB's out," Ella announced, her breath visible in the cold air as she held the phone to her ear. "We'll have eyes everywhere looking for her."

"Good," Priscilla nodded, her gaze sweeping across the disarray once more before something caught her attention—a small picture frame hanging on a wall between two bookshelves. She walked towards it, her curiosity piqued.

"Hey, Ella, come take a look at this," Priscilla called, beckoning her over with a wave of her hand. Ella obliged, curiosity etched on her face.

"What is it?" Ella asked, peering at the picture. In it, a modest cabin nestled among snow-capped mountains. The sun cast a warm glow over the scene, creating a stark contrast to their current surroundings.

"Margaret might have gone here," Priscilla proposed, her forehead creased with thought. "She was spooked, right? What better place to hide than a secluded cabin?"

"Could be..." Ella murmured, studying the photograph. She imagined Margaret fleeing her home, heart pounding, and seeking refuge in the isolated cabin. It made sense, but something gnawed at her gut, telling her there was more to this. Who had called? Who had scared her? And were they on their way now... to do something worse?

"Okay, let's say she's there," Ella said, her voice firm and decisive. "We need to find out where this cabin is located."

"Right," Priscilla agreed, pulling out her phone. "I'll see if I can find anything about it online."

As Priscilla tapped away on her phone, Ella couldn't shake the unease that settled over her like a heavy fog. The frigid Alaskan air nipped at her skin, but it was the thought of Margaret—alone and terrified—that sent shivers down her spine.

"Please let us find her in time," Ella whispered to herself, her breath leaving a visible trail in the frosty air. The urgency weighed heavily upon her as she waited for Priscilla to uncover any information that could lead them to Margaret's potential hiding place.

"Got it!" Priscilla exclaimed, her eyes widening with excitement. "I found a listing on her social profile about the cabin. It's her family's retreat, up in the mountains—about an hour from here."

"Then we don't have a moment to lose," Ella declared, determination surging through her veins. She had no idea what awaited them at that cabin, but she knew they couldn't waste any more time.

"Let's go," Priscilla agreed, already heading towards the door.

As she turned to follow Priscilla out, something caught her eye—a gun locker tucked away in the corner, its door slightly ajar.

"Wait, Priscilla," Ella called out, her voice tense. She approached the gun locker, noticing that it had been left unlocked. Her fingers traced the edges of the empty slots where firearms should have been resting. "Margaret took her guns with her. All of them."

"Are you sure?" Priscilla asked, concern etching her features as she joined Ella by the locker.

"Positive." Ella closed the locker softly, her mind racing with possibilities. *Why would Margaret arm herself like this? What kind of danger was she in?*

"Let's get going, then," Priscilla urged, her eyes meeting Ella's with shared determination.

They moved quickly, stepping out into the biting Alaskan air and making their way towards the car. The wind howled around them, whipping up flurries of snow that danced through the beams of the car's headlights. She beat her sister to the front seat this time, and Ella started the engine, feeling the subtle vibration beneath her fingertips as the vehicle roared to life.

"An hour," Priscilla said, glancing at her phone for directions. "We've got a long drive ahead of us."

"Every second counts," Ella replied, shifting gears and accelerating onto the desolate road. The snow crunched beneath the tires as they sped away from Margaret's home, leaving only tire tracks in their wake.

As they drove, Ella's thoughts churned like the turbulent sea outside, the waves crashing against the frozen shoreline. *What could have scared Margaret so badly that she fled to the mountains, armed to the teeth?* She gripped the steering wheel tighter, her knuckles turning white from the pressure.

"Hey," Priscilla's voice cut through Ella's thoughts. "Don't mess this up, okay?"

"Whatever, Cilla."

"Whatever right back. We'll find her—she'll help us figure out what she saw live, and we'll find those creeps who did the governor. Simple." She nodded resolutely.

Ella gave a tight nod, her eyes never leaving the road ahead. "I hope you're right, Priscilla. I really do."

The darkness of the night seemed to swallow them whole as they continued their journey into the heart of the Alaskan wilderness, chasing after shadows.

Chapter 6

The man smiled like a shark and barely sweated as he moved with the precision of a master craftsman. He stood in the center of the dimly lit room, flanked by two larger opponents. Sweat glistened on their bulky frames as they sized up their formidable adversary. The air was thick with tension, anticipation crackling like static electricity.

"Come on," the man growled, beckoning his challengers. His eyes bore into them, cold and unyielding. "Show me. *Now.*" His was a voice of authority. A demanding voice that required instant compliance.

And comply they did... they always did.

The first opponent lunged forward, muscles rippling beneath his tattooed skin. But the man of authority was faster. With a deft sidestep, he grabbed the attacker's arm, twisting it behind his back in a swift Ju-jitsu maneuver. The man let out a howl of pain before being sent crashing to the floor with a thud that echoed throughout the chamber.

"Is that all?" the Architect said, his icy gaze never leaving the second opponent. "Or do you have more to offer? A deal requires sacrifice."

The remaining challenger grit his teeth as he charged headlong at the Architect. But the man was ready for him, too. He ducked under the attacker's swing, using his own momentum to flip him over his shoulder and onto the ground. As the second opponent writhed in agony, the Architect locked his arm around the man's neck, applying just enough pressure to make his point.

"Yield," the Architect commanded, his voice low and dangerous. It wasn't a question. They'd seen what he'd done to those who *refused* to yield.

"Fine! I yield!" gasped his defeated opponent, bloodshot eyes bulging with panic and defeat. The Architect released his grip, allowing the man to slump to the floor, gasping for breath.

Standing between the defeated, the Architect's face remained eerily expressionless—a side effect of the numerous plastic surgeries he had undergone to render his visage unreadable.

Glancing down at the two defeated opponents, the Architect raised an eyebrow. He then turned and approached a live-edge wood bench where he bent over and picked up his personal belongings, slowly affixing them.

In that moment, they all noticed the subtle indicators of his wealth: a glint of his gold cufflinks beneath the sleeves of his tailored suit which lay folded on the bench, the sleek watch that now hugged his wrist, and the way he carried himself with an air of untouchable confidence.

"So," said the Architect, his plastic features remaining impassive and unreadable, "Do we understand each other?"

The two men groaned, pushing up from the ground. Two more body-guards stood by the doors, carrying weapons and doing their best to appear intimidating. No difficult proposition given the Uzi submachine guns holstered over their shoulders.

The Architect glanced back at the two fallen men, "I said do we understand each other?"

The two thugs blinked in confusion.

He sighed. "Shooting someone isn't part of the game. I was clear about that. It's boring." He said. "Have a little panache."

Both men nodded urgently.

"Y-yes," stammered the first burly man, clearly intimidated. "We won't shoot no one again. Swear it."

"Good," the Architect replied curtly, moving towards the exit. As he walked, he couldn't help but think about how easily they had crumbled. *Amateurs*, he mused to himself.

"So... we're allowed to go? You ain't gonna... feed us to nuffin are you?"

"Fine," the Architect responded, offering a dispassionate smile. Though it was difficult to read his thoughts, there was no mistaking the satisfaction that filled him.

He turned away from the two men. They would live. For now. While it was true they'd broken the first rule of the game... they'd used firearms in their kills, the targets they'd chosen had been amusing. An old lady they'd snatched from outside a storefront. And a teenage girl who'd been walking home from school.

He nodded in appreciation. It was the vulnerable that society most wept for.

He turned away from his two rueful sparring opponents.

The Architect stepped out of the dimly lit room, his expressionless face like a mask, betraying no emotion. His cold eyes surveyed the well-manicured airfield before him, a stark contrast to the chaos he had just left behind. The sun was setting, casting an orange glow that bathed the tarmac in warm hues.

The sound of hurrying footsteps indicated the approaching man. A figure stepped forward with hasty motions.

"Your private jet is ready for takeoff, sir," said a uniformed pilot, snapping a sharp salute.

"Thank you," the Architect replied, his tone even and detached. As he approached the sleek aircraft waiting for him, its gleaming fuselage reflecting the waning sunlight, he couldn't help but appreciate the luxury it represented—a fitting reward for his hard work and success.

Just as he neared the plane's entrance, a figure stumbled into view from around the corner of a nearby hangar. It was a man, seemingly battered and bruised, with one arm hanging limply at his side. The Architect froze, examining the intruder with calculating scrutiny. *Who is this?*

"Wait!" the figure said, his voice ragged. Recognition dawned—a tanned man with tattoos. A killer who'd been sent to Nome. But now he was *here*?

"Speak," the Architect commanded, his demeanor unyielding. He subtly shifted his weight, ready to defend himself if necessary.

Geo? Leo? What was his name... The Architect couldn't remember.

"I need... I need to disappear," said the man quickly.

The Architect raised an eyebrow. "You know better than to come here, don't you?"

"Yeah... yeah, shit, but look at me! They killed him." His voice choked. "They killed my brother."

The would-be assassin had a panicked look in his eyes, and it wasn't becoming at all.

"Your point?" the Architect asked coldly.

"I... look, I did what you asked. But she has backup. travels with this US Marshal." The man winced, shrugging.

"I still don't think we've addressed why you're *here*."

The Architect's icy tone caused the assassin to tremble. "Roderick," the Architect said quietly, "That's your name, isn't it?"

The man began to frown and shake his head no.

"Roderick it is," the Architect said. "You really shouldn't have come here, but you are proving something I've known. If one wants something done properly, one must do it themselves, hmm? But fine. I'll help you disappear."

As Roderick's guard dropped ever so slightly in relief, the Architect seized the opportunity. With calculated precision, he launched a rapid strike aimed at the assassin's throat, his fingers forming a lethal weapon.

Roderick's eyes widened in shock, but before he could react, the Architect's hand connected with his windpipe, crushing it instantly. He collapsed to the ground, gasping for breath that would never come.

The Architect watched dispassionately as Roderick's body spasmed, his desperate attempts to draw air growing weaker and weaker. *One less potential threat,* he thought coldly. His ruthlessness had always been his greatest asset, and he had no intention of letting that change now.

As Roderick's life drained from his body, the Architect turned away, already focused on his next move.

He paused, though, and glanced back.

"Such a waste," he murmured, almost tenderly, as he bent over to pull the laces free from the man's shoes. "You could have been so much more, Roderick."

The pilot was still standing off to the side, his face stony, refusing to look over.

The Architect glanced up, his surgically enhanced face betraying no emotion. "A ritual," he explained, twirling the freshly removed laces between his fingers. "I like to take a piece of them with me."

"R-right..." the man stuttered, swallowing hard, still staring ahead at the plane.

"Tell me," the Architect continued, rising to his feet. "What do you see when you look at these laces?"

"Uh, just... shoelaces, sir?" the man replied hesitantly.

"Hmm, oh well." One by one, the Architect wrapped the laces around his wrist, joining the countless others already adorning it. "To most, they're nothing but ordinary shoelaces. But to me, they represent something far greater."

"Y-yes, sir," the man stammered.

With that, the Architect made his way toward the waiting plane, whistling a tune that seemed oddly cheerful considering the circumstances. As he walked, his thoughts turned to his next target: Jameson Porter.

"Mr. Porter," he whispered under his breath, a dangerous edge to his voice. "Your time is running out." The Architect could already imagine the satisfaction of adding Jameson's shoelaces to his collection, another symbol of a job well done.

His private jet loomed before him, an imposing figure against the sky. As he climbed the stairs to the aircraft, his determination only grew stronger, fueled by the knowledge that each step brought him closer to his ultimate goal.

"Jameson Porter," he said once more, the name rolling off his tongue like a promise.

Chapter 7

The mountain cabin stood isolated and solemn, nestled within the icy cradle of a treacherous ravine. Surrounded by jagged cliffs and a dense forest of pines, its weather-beaten facade bore witness to countless winter storms. The small, dilapidated structure barely provided shelter from the biting wind that whipped through the air, carrying a flurry of snowflakes that danced like ghosts in the moonlight.

Ella shivered, her breath misting in front of her as she gazed at the cabin. Her blonde hair was pulled back into a tight ponytail. Her piercing blue eyes scanned their surroundings, always alert to potential danger.

"Are you sure this is the place?" Ella asked, her voice a taut wire stretched thin over her suspicions.

Priscilla stood beside her, a stark contrast to Ella's cautious presence. Priscilla was pacing agitatedly, glaring up at the cabin like a pit-bull on too long of a leash. "The GPS wouldn't have brought you here if it wasn't," she replied coolly, her gaze unwavering.

Ella massaged her gloved hands together, attempting to restore warmth and feeling to her numb fingers.

As they approached the cabin, Ella couldn't help but feel the weight of the danger that lurked around them, clinging to the air like the frost on her eyelashes.

"Stay behind me," Ella instructed, her voice betraying no hint of her internal struggle. "We don't know what we'll find in there."

Priscilla nodded, her expression inscrutable. Together, they trudged through the deep snow, each step an arduous battle against the unforgiving terrain. The wind shrieked its discontent, as if warning them of the perils that lay ahead. And yet, despite the looming threats and unspoken doubts, the two women pressed onward—drawn together by a shared purpose as they ventured into the heart of danger.

The steep incline loomed ahead of them, a daunting challenge made even more treacherous by the thick layer of snow that blanketed the ground. Each step up the slope was a battle as their boots sank into the icy powder, their legs straining against the weight of their bodies and the relentless pull of gravity. Wind battered their faces, stinging exposed skin and threatening to throw them off balance.

"Damn it," Ella muttered under her breath, gritting her teeth as she dug her gloved hands into the snow for any semblance of grip. "This is worse than I thought."

Priscilla, just behind her, grunted in agreement.

Ella glanced back at her companion, scrutinizing her wariness.

As they neared the top of the incline, Ella's heart leaped into her throat. She spotted a faint light flickering from within the cabin. The hair on the back of her neck prickled with a sudden surge of adrenaline.

"Wait here," she whispered to Priscilla, though, it was a longshot that Cilla would listen to the instruction. With careful steps, Ella approached the cabin, feeling a mixture of dread and anticipation pooling in her gut.

Preparing to announce herself, Ella's words caught in her throat as her eyes met the vague gaze of a shadowy figure through the window. Not a woman... a man, and he was glaring right toward them.

"Get down!" Ella hissed at Priscilla, her heart pounding in her chest. She could feel the tension between them, charged like an electric current.

"Who's there?" a gruff voice called out from inside the cabin. Definitely not Margaret's voice.

"Damn," Ella muttered under her breath, cursing herself for not approaching more discreetly. Her mind raced as she tried to formulate a response that would buy them time.

"Lost hikers," she called back, praying the ruse would work. "Our group got separated in the storm."

"Stay where you are!" the voice ordered. "Don't come any closer."

Ella glanced back at Priscilla with wide eyes, the weight of their mission pressing down on her. They needed to get inside that cabin, and this unexpected obstacle threatened everything they'd worked for.

"Listen," she began, trying to sound calm and reasonable, "we're freezing out here, and we just need some shelter until the storm passes. Can you help us?"

"Last chance!" the voice barked, clearly unconvinced. "Turn around and leave now!"

Ella's heart raced as she tried to think of a way to defuse the situation. As her mind grasped at possibilities, suddenly, the sharp crack of a gunshot split the air, the sound echoing through the frozen landscape. The bullet whizzed past her ear, missing her by mere inches. Instinctively, she threw herself to the side, adrenaline coursing through her veins.

"Run!" she shouted to Priscilla, her survival instincts taking over. As she scrambled away from the cabin, her foot slipped on the edge of the steep incline, sending her tumbling toward the precipice below.

The ground was treacherous, and what she'd thought was solid footing was just open, white powder.

Her hands flailed wildly, desperate for something to hold onto. Just as she thought she would be swallowed by the darkness below, her gloved fingers closed around a jutting root that protruded from the snowy ground.

"Priscilla!" she gasped, her muscles straining to maintain her grip on the root. Her body dangled over the cliff, the wind whipping at her hair and stinging her face with icy tendrils.

Her sister's name came out as a gasp of exertion, her strength waning as the reality of her situation threatened to overwhelm her.

"Hang on, Ella!" Priscilla shouted, already scrambling toward her. Ella forced herself to focus on her partner's voice, using it as an anchor in the chaos that surrounded them.

As she clung to life on the edge of the abyss, Ella's thoughts raced through every possible outcome, each more terrifying than the last.

Ella's leg twisted unnaturally as it became trapped between two jagged rocks, the pain searing through her like a hot knife. She bit back a scream, her breaths coming in shallow gasps from both fear and agony. Her body trembled with the effort to hold on to the root and keep her weight off her injured limb.

"Priscilla!" she cried out again, her voice weak but urgent.

There was another gunshot, but no sound of impact as the snow muffled the retort.

"Damn it, Ella!" Priscilla hissed through gritted teeth as she dropped to her knees at the edge of the cliff.

"Less talking, more helping!" Ella retorted, her desperation fueling the anger that bubbled beneath the surface. She knew that their relationship had been tense lately, but now was not the time for recriminations.

Priscilla muttered, her gaze darting around to assess the situation. "I'm going to reach down and grab your arm. You need to let go of the root and trust me."

"Trust you?" Ella couldn't help the incredulous laugh that escaped her lips, despite the precariousness of her position. "Yeah, because that's worked out so well for us lately."

"Dammit, Ella! This isn't the time!" Priscilla snapped, her frustration evident. "Just give me your hand!"

Ella hesitated for a moment, the memories of their recent arguments threatening to cloud her judgment. But she couldn't afford to dwell on that now. With a deep, shuddering breath, she released the root and reached up toward Priscilla.

Ella's heart pounded in her chest, her fingers numb from the cold and fear. She stared into Priscilla's eyes, searching for any sign of the trust they once shared. The wind whipped around them, howling like a malevolent force bent on prying her loose from the cliffside. Her fingers brushed against Priscilla's glove, their connection tenuous at first but then growing stronger as Priscilla tightened her grip.

"Come on, Ella!" Priscilla gritted her teeth, her muscles tensing as she strained to pull Ella back up the incline. She grunted with effort, her jaw set in determination, refusing to let go.

Ella felt her own strength returning, fueled by a mixture of gratitude and adrenaline. Together, they fought against gravity and the treacherous terrain, inch by painstaking inch.

As they neared the top of the ledge, Priscilla's grip never wavered, and Ella couldn't help but feel a sense of relief wash over her as she stumbled onto the edge of the cliff, safe.

No sooner had they caught their breath than a sudden cacophony of gunfire erupted, echoing through the mountain air. Ella's instincts kicked in instantly, her eyes darting around as she scanned the area for the source of the shots.

"Down!" Priscilla yelled, her voice tight with urgency as she pushed Ella behind a snow-covered boulder near the cabin.

"Where are they?" Ella whispered, her heart pounding in her chest.

"Over there, at the tree line," Priscilla answered, pointing across the clearing.

Ella squinted into the distance and saw faint shadows darting between the trees, their outlines obscured by the thick curtain of falling snow. Two more men, both of them rushing to the cabin. She cursed under her breath—these shooters were smart, using the weather to their advantage, obscuring their movements.

"Stay low. We need to make it to the cabin," Priscilla said, determination etched on her face.

"Are you insane?" Ella couldn't believe what she was hearing, but before she could protest further, Priscilla grabbed her arm and yanked her forward.

"Trust me!" Priscilla insisted, and despite the lingering tension between them, Ella knew she had no choice.

As bullets whizzed past them, the two women scrambled from one makeshift cover to another, their breaths labored in the freezing air. Fear gnawed at Ella's insides, but she pushed it down, focusing instead on the rhythmic sound of her own heartbeat and the reassuring grip of Priscilla's hand on hers.

"Ready?" Priscilla asked, her eyes locked on the cabin door just a few yards away.

"Let's go." Ella steeled herself, knowing this final sprint would be their most dangerous yet.

As they charged toward the door, more gunfire erupted from the tree line, the deadly projectiles tearing through the snow like angry hornets. Ella could feel the icy burn of adrenaline coursing through her veins, but she refused to give in to the panic threatening to consume her. She had come too far, survived too much, to be taken out now.

Barely a foot away from the door, Ella felt her ankle catch on something and sent her tumbling to the ground. The impact knocked the wind out of her, and for a moment, the world went black.

"Priscilla!" she gasped, fear gripping her as she realized she'd lost her grip on her sister's hand.

"Get inside!" Priscilla shouted, her voice barely audible over the gunfire. She was standing over Ella, providing cover as she strained to reach the cabin door.

As she fumbled with the handle, Ella felt a bullet whiz past her ear, so close she could almost feel its heat. Panic surged through her, and she knew she had only seconds left before their luck ran out.

"Come on, come on..." she muttered, willing the door to open. And then, suddenly, it did.

"Get in!" Priscilla pushed Ella through the doorway, and together they stumbled into the relative safety of the cabin. As the door slammed shut behind them, the sound of gunfire continued to ring out, a chilling reminder of the danger lurking just beyond the walls, from the line of the trees.

The two other men hadn't reached the cabin in time, and now they were circling back to a shed behind the cabin, shouting at each other.

But as Ella looked around the dimly lit room, her relief at escaping the hail of bullets was short-lived, replaced by a sinking feeling of dread.

For there, in the shadows, stood the figure of the man she'd seen from below.

"Drop the gun!" Cilla barked, pointing her weapon at the man.

He stared at them both, eyes narrowed. Then he cursed, raising his own weapon and opening fire.

Chapter 8

The gunman in the cabin opened fire but a second too late.

Cilla moved first.

Her giant hand cannon shot up; she squeezed the trigger twice.

The gunman's bullets went wide from the impact of being shot. Two blossoms of red spread across his checkered shirt, and his mouth opened and closed, his eyes widening in horror as he stumbled back.

The man hit the wall and slid down, his gun falling from his hand as his body went limp. Ella stared in horror but could taste adrenaline overwhelming her senses.

Cilla approached and stood over the man's body, gun still trained on him, her expression unreadable. "It had to be done," she said, her voice steady but cold.

She glanced back at Ella. "By my count, that's twice I've saved your life. *Today.*"

Ella could only nod mutely, a million thoughts racing through her mind. The cabin was empty aside from the dead man.

No sign of Margaret.

She frowned, though, a sudden lull in the gunfire giving her pause as she peered through the window looking toward the shed.

No movement.

"Where did they go?"

"The two shooters?"

A nod.

Cilla just shrugged. "Didn't see."

Ella cursed, peering towards the wood shed. It was about the size of a single-car garage, with a window perched on top of the roof in a sort of triangular frame.

She spotted a large oak tree adjacent to the shed, its sturdy branches reaching out towards the roof.

"Cover me," Ella said suddenly.

"What are you—"

But now it was Ella's turn to ignore her sister's comments. With practiced agility, Ella dashed towards the tree, her boots crunching on the forest floor. She circled around the side of the cabin, avoiding line of sight from the shed's windows.

Her body moved with the fluidity of a seasoned athlete.

Ella leaped at the lowest branch, fingers curling around the rough bark. The strain in her forearms reminded her of countless hours spent training for moments like this. She swung her legs up and over, using her momentum to propel herself onto the next branch. Vertigo threatened to unbalance her, but she refused to let it take hold.

Sweat beaded on her brow despite the cold of the Alaskan mountain as she navigated the maze of branches above her.

The howl of the wind had reached a crescendo as she reached the final branch; she extended her arm, fingertips brushing against the weathered shingles of the shed's roof.

She gritted her teeth as she hurled herself towards the edge.

Her fingers grasped the shingles just in time, her body slamming against the side of the shed. Pain shot through her ribs, but she bit back a cry, knowing that any sound could give her away. With one final heave, she hoisted herself onto the roof, her chest heaving as adrenaline coursed through her veins.

Ella crawled across the rough shingles, feeling the grit dig into her palms as she approached what looked to be a small attic window. Not a shed then. A garage? With an attic? She carefully pried it open with a pocket knife, wincing as the hinges creaked. Her heart pounded in her chest like a jackhammer, but she took a deep breath to steady herself before hoisting herself through the narrow opening.

The room was dimly lit by slats of sunlight that pierced through curtains that billowed softly in the breeze from the open window. Dust motes danced in the air, and Ella could make out the faint outline of an old bookshelf and a desk cluttered with papers. An office above the garage. She could smell the scent of fuel and grease coming from below. But her attention was immediately drawn to the man perched next to another window at the far end of the room.

She grimaced, observing his military-style haircut and cold, steely eyes. His tense posture, the sniper rifle cradled expertly in his hands, told her all she needed to know: this man was a professional.

He was peering through the other window, eyes on his scope, sighting towards the cabin. He hadn't spotted her yet.

She took a hesitant step towards him. A floorboard creaked.

The sniper's head snapped towards her, his eyes narrowing as he assessed the situation. The slightest shift in his weight as he hesitated, caught off guard by her sudden appearance.

And then he raised his rifle.

She didn't have time to hesitate. Her own gun snapped to attention.

A single shot.

He spun like a top, falling to the ground. She'd winged him. He was groaning, so she hastened over, kicking his rifle away and cuffing him to the radiator. "Don't move," she said. "Keep pressure on that or you'll bleed out." She'd have to make sure the local PD picked him up at some point, but for now, she had other concerns.

With the sniper handcuffed and temporarily out of commission, Ella scanned the dimly lit room, her heart pounding in her chest. She knew she needed to find Margaret quickly, but there was no time to waste on fear or hesitation. The room seemed empty other than a bed, a dresser, and a door that led to a hallway. She could hear muffled voices coming from downstairs, and she knew that was where she needed to be.

"Please let Margaret be okay," Ella whispered under her breath as she stepped into the hallway and cautiously approached the top of the stairs. She gripped her gun tightly, feeling its weight in her hand like an anchor grounding her in this chaotic moment.

She descended the staircase, each step creaking beneath her careful weight. As she reached the landing, her pulse quickened when she spotted a man standing at the foot of the stairs staring straight up at her.

He cursed and raised his gun, but she squeezed her own trigger first, the gunshot ringing out like a thunderclap in the confined space. The man's eyes widened in shock as he stumbled back, clutching at the red stain blossoming on his chest.

There was no time for remorse when Margaret's life was still hanging in the balance. She sprinted down the remaining steps, pushing onward toward the chaos that awaited her.

As Ella reached the bottom of the stairs, her eyes locked onto the figure tied to a wooden chair near an old tractor in the center of the garage.

She blinked and then let out a small exhalation.

"Shit."

Margaret Whitaker was tied to a chair.

Her throat was slit.

Chapter 9

Ella and Priscilla stood side by side, staring at the body tied to the chair.

Ella didn't say a word, but breathing heavily, inhaling the coppery scent of blood, she reached for her pocket and pulled out her phone. She cycled to the DMV photo they'd been provided of Margaret.

"Is it a match?" Cilla said, her voice hoarse. A bloom of white mist extended from her lips, carried by the cold air behind them.

Ella just nodded once, her hand going limp as she lowered her phone.

"Shit," Priscilla said, cursing and turning away from the body of their would-be witness.

She kicked the gunman she'd shot as she turned, glaring at his fallen, bleeding form.

"They torture her?" Cilla said, turning away from the body now as if she might be sick.

Ella nodded again. "Looks like it."

"Why the hell?"

"I don't know," Ella murmured. She frowned, taking a step towards the body, shivering as she did. The echo of gunshots had now faded.

She leaned in, studying the woman tied to the chair. "She's missing a tooth..." Ella murmured.

"What?" Cilla turned following Ella's finger as she pointed to Margaret's mouth, frozen in a rictus of pain from her final moments.

A dark gap winked out from between otherwise healthy-looking teeth, and though forensics wasn't Ella's specialty, the signs were clear that whoever took the missing tooth had been none too gentle in the process. But why? Part of the torture? A trophy?

Shaking her head, Ella stepped back. "They lured her here," she said, her attention returning to the queries on her phone. "Whoever placed that phone call... they lured her."

"Any luck on that number?"

"None. Burner."

"*Shit*," Cilla said again, emphasizing the word this time.

The two of them both went quiet.

Ella tried not to stare at Margaret, as if somehow it was a taboo thing for her to look at the dead woman.

She could feel her heart twisting in her chest, her blood pumping rapidly.

"What the hell's going on here, Ella?" Cilla said.

Ella glanced at her sister. The two of them locked gazes.

"I don't know."

"Bullshit."

"I don't know, Cilla."

"Like hell you don't! Three gunmen hunt down a woman from Nome? You don't even bat an eyelid. *What* the hell is going on?" This time, Cilla stepped forward, jabbing her finger hard against her sister's shoulder.

Ella took a step back, relieved to have an excuse to look away from the corpse.

"I saved your life," Cilla added, firmly. "Twice." She held up two fingers, then used these to jab at her sister again.

"I know," Ella said, murmuring softly. Her mind was whirring. She thought of the Architect, the Collective. Someone had murdered the governor, and now they wanted to kill Ella's father.

Did Cilla deserve to know?

She hesitated only briefly then let out a slow breath, the air seeping from her lips like the blood pooling on the floor. She frowned at her sister, tense.

And then, in a soft voice, she said, "The Collective."

"Excuse me?" Cilla demanded, leaning in.

"It's the Collective," Ella said.

Cilla froze. She hesitated briefly, licking her lips nervously. "The what?"

"Don't act like you don't know. You're the one who told me."

Priscilla stared at her sister, and then her eyes narrowed.

"When you were in the hospital, remember?" Ella said quietly.

Priscilla shook her head. "What the hell are you involved with, Ella?"

Ella crossed her arms. She tried not to allow a frown to curdle her features. Her sister, on the other hand, had no such aversion.

"I'm not the one who tampered with this, Cilla. Dad did."

"Of course. Of course you're going to blame him!"

"I'm not *blaming* anyone. I'm explaining. Dad is involved with them, Cilla."

"He's not some psycho, Ella."

"I don't mean he's one of their members. But he kept records on them. He knew about them. I think that's why they're coming after him."

The two sisters frowned at each other, though Ella's expression flickered back into an impassive, polite facade far quicker than her sister's. Cilla's, on the other hand, smoldered like the fuse of a stick of dynamite.

"So you kicked over a damn hornet's nest, and now people are dead?" Cilla demanded, waving a hand towards Margaret's corpse.

"No... I followed a lead and tugged on a thread. Dad's the one who brought this on Nome."

Cilla was just shaking her head now, muttering under her breath. She approached the gunman she'd shot and began rifling through his pockets.

"What are you doing?" Ella demanded.

"What does it look like, Sherlock?"

Cilla produced a wallet. "I'm looking for something that might give us a lead on these guys." She flipped open the wallet and pulled out a driver's license.

"Benny Polinski," she said. "Recognize the name?"

"No," Ella replied, her eyes scanning the area for anything that might give them more information. She noticed a small, black box sitting on a nearby table and hesitated for only a moment before approaching it.

"Benny Polinski," Cilla repeated slowly, giving the license a final disheartened stare. "I don't recognize him either," she said, stuffing the wallet into her back pocket.

Ella reached out and grabbed the box. She turned it over in her hands, examining it closely. She noticed that there was a small, glass opening on the front of the box.

She froze.

"What?" Cilla said. "What is it?"

"A camera," Ella said quietly, frowning down at the device. A small, green light blinked next to the lens, watching her.

She felt a shiver crawl down her spine.

She placed the camera back on the table and realized it had been faced towards Margaret in her chair.

"Someone... someone was watching them torture her," Ella whispered.

"Shit... *Shit*! If you really did hear about the Collective, you would know they're a bunch of assholes. Killers, Ella. Real bastards. And now they're coming after Dad!"

"They killed the governor, Cilla. They're on the move. I don't even know why... but they're playing at something."

Cilla was pacing now. "So... So, a secret society of serial killers... funded by a billionaire, I might add, go after the governor. Kill him brazenly on live TV. And now... they want Dad? Because he owns a gold mine?"

"Because he's corrupt?" Ella muttered under her breath.

Cilla flung the wallet at her sister, and Ella dodged it. As she did, though, there was a *clicking* sound as the wallet hit the ground.

Ella frowned, turning back around.

Cilla hadn't noticed. But Ella bent over, picking up the wallet, and rubbing her fingers over a bump in the fabric, ignoring her sister who was lecturing Ella for disloyalty once more.

She'd heard it all before and wasn't particularly interested in hearing more.

Now, though, as Ella stared at the wallet in her hand, her thumb rubbing over the back, she pulled a knife from her pocket.

The knife worked the fabric away, and Ella plucked a tiny metal mechanism from the wallet.

A thin antennae stuck out from it, and a slow, steady, strobing pinprick of light pulsed from the small screen.

"Tracking device," Ella said.

Cilla glanced over. She frowned and approached cautiously. The twins stared at the small device.

"You're sure?" Cilla asked.

"Yeah. I recognize it. It's a GPS tracker. Same sort we've used on CIs during busts."

Cilla sucked in a sharp breath, her eyes wide. "So they know where their guys are? Know we've killed them?"

"It seems that way," Ella replied, slipping the device into her pocket. "We need to get out of here. Now."

"You're just keeping that?"

"Might be able to reverse engineer the signal."

"What?"

Ella just shrugged. "Dunno. Worth keeping, though."

"Can't we turn it off or something?"

Ella nodded. "Already did."

"Oh. Good, then."

But of course, Ella was lying.

She hadn't turned off the device. She needed it to continue. Needed *them* to come to *her*.

Whoever was behind all this, they'd killed the governor of a US state. They'd gone on to murder one of the witnesses. But why?

Why target Margaret?

Unless, of course, it was just more taunting. Letting the police know that it didn't matter *what* they did. That the Collective was always one step ahead.

Ella felt a slow shiver down her back.

She glanced through the shattered glass behind her where bullets had allowed cold wind to rush through. The dark of night had settled quickly. The cold continued to threaten them. Flurries of snow were now sweeping across snowdrifts leading up to the cabin.

"I'll call it in. Then we should head back," Ella said quietly.

Cilla was shaking her head, scowling at the ground. "We need to get to Dad."

"Mhmm..."

All the while, Ella could feel the outline of the live tracking device in her pocket. Someone wanted to keep an eye on their gunmen.

That same someone would wonder what had happened. Perhaps would come looking.

And when they did...

Ella would be waiting.

Chapter 10

The Architect was wearing sweats now and a bright, pink hoodie. He had earbuds in and was listening to his new favorite indie artist.

His head bobbed in time with the music, and his dark, black bangs shifted across his eyes.

Of course, his hair wasn't *normally* this color, but like his features, his hair had also seen some work.

He jogged along the harbor, whistling as he did, and keeping pace with the small boat two hundred yards off-shore that seemed to follow him.

The three men in the boat were grim-faced. The woman in the back looked tense, her face as rigid as it would be if it were carved from granite.

The Architect continued to jog along the shore, humming in time with the soft dulcet tones of banjo and guitar strings.

He wore earmuffs, also pink, and bright, orange running shoes.

He had on an oversized sweatband and goggles that fogged up as he ran.

He knew he looked like some dorky suburban dad out for a run in the cold, harsh climate of Nome, Alaska, but that was intentional.

Most of what he did was intentional.

He'd decided to handle *this* personally.

Running along the waterfront, the Architect took in the salty breeze mixed with the scent of fresh fish from a nearby market. Though he had arrived at a private airfield just an hour ago, he wasted no time in *executing*.

Parallel to him, the 30-foot speedboat glided through the water, barely creating a ripple. Its sleek design and matte black paint job made it almost invisible against the darkening harbor, though it stood out in Nome. Most of the vessels here were fisherman boats, old dredges, or rusted hunks of wood and metal. But the Architect spared no expense. Onboard, the three bodyguards, dressed in black suits and sunglasses, surveyed their surroundings. They were instructed to shadow the Architect while maintaining their distance, so as not to raise suspicion. Their eyes, hidden behind mirrored lenses, never strayed far from their charge.

"Keep your eyes open, gentlemen. We don't want any surprises," said the Architect through the wireless earbud nestled in his ear, his voice calm and collected.

"Understood, sir," replied the lead bodyguard, his gaze fixed on the shore where the Architect jogged.

As the Architect continued his run, he observed the surrounding area, mentally cataloging every detail. Each observation brought him one step closer to his ultimate goal—Jameson Porter.

"Perfectly positioned lampposts, wide streets, limited access points... this place has been well thought-out," he mused, his satisfaction evident.

"Sir, we've noticed increased security around the perimeter," reported the second bodyguard from the boat.

"Excellent," the Architect responded, a small smile playing at the corner of his lips. "That means we're on the right track. Let's keep going and see what else we can find."

"Copy that, sir," acknowledged the third bodyguard.

The Architect couldn't help but feel a thrill at the challenge before him. As he jogged along the harbor, his thoughts raced, already devising a plan to outwit his opponents and achieve his objective. The more difficult the task, the more exhilarating the payoff.

The rhythmic pounding of the Architect's shoes against the pavement filled his ears as he approached the government safehouse. From a distance, it was an inconspicuous building nestled between two larger structures. But the Architect knew better—behind its unassuming façade lay secrets and power, the allure of which had drawn him here.

"Safehouse is in sight," he informed his bodyguards through the wireless earbuds. "Remember, I'm just a jogger passing by."

"Understood, sir," replied the lead bodyguard.

As the Architect drew closer to the safehouse, he adjusted the volume on his music, letting the thumping bassline wash over him. The casual onlooker would simply see a man absorbed in his run. Anyone familiar with the Architect, however, would recognize his ability to multitask—enjoying his music while mentally taking snapshots of the safehouse and its surroundings.

"Six o'clock," murmured the Architect into his earbud, noting the position of a uniformed police officer lounging against a patrol car. "And another at three o'clock, chatting with a private security guard."

"Copy that, sir," acknowledged the second bodyguard from the speedboat.

"Two more on the rooftop," the Architect added, his eyes scanning the horizon with laser-like precision. "Excellent vantage points."

"Got it, sir," responded the third bodyguard.

The Architect took a deep breath, feeling the salt-tinged air fill his lungs. He could feel the adrenaline coursing through his veins as the challenge before him solidified. It was time to put his plan into action.

"Stay sharp, gentlemen. This is where the real fun begins," he said, a hint of excitement in his voice.

"Ready when you are, sir," affirmed the lead bodyguard.

With each stride, the Architect's mind raced, piecing together a mental map of the safehouse and its defenses. It was a formidable fortress, but he had a knack for finding the cracks in any armor. And as he ran past the unassuming building, he couldn't help but smile.

The Architect's eyes narrowed as he assessed the safehouse's defenses. A pair of armed men in an unmarked black SUV cruised past, their vigilance palpable even through the dark, tinted windows. He cataloged them in his mental inventory alongside the seven police officers and four private security personnel scattered around the perimeter.

"Two more in a black SUV," he relayed to his team through his earpiece. "Keep an eye out for them."

"Understood, sir," came the response from his lead bodyguard.

As the Architect continued jogging, his breathing remained steady and controlled. He was a master of his own body, able to push himself physically while maintaining the mental acuity necessary to execute his intricate plans.

"Tell me the stakes don't thrill you," he whispered to himself, a smile playing at the corners of his mouth. The challenge ahead invigorated him, and he reveled in that sensation.

"Sir?" asked one of his bodyguards, catching the comment over the earpiece.

"Nothing," the Architect replied dismissively, refocusing on the task at hand. "Just enjoying the game."

His gaze swept across the waterfront, noting every detail—the way the waves lapped against the dock, the rustle of wind through the nearby trees, the rhythm of his footfalls on the pavement. Each piece of information coalesced into a vivid mosaic of the mission before him.

The SUV trundling past paused. It began to turn, heading towards him.

"Pick me up," he said, barely moving his lips. "The canaries are curious."

He darted down an alleyway opposite the safehouse, his tracksuit-clad frame melding seamlessly with the shadows. The worn cobblestones beneath his feet were slick with moisture, but the Architect moved with agility and grace, his focus never wavering.

As he emerged from the alley, the wharf came into view. Seagulls squawked overhead, diving towards discarded scraps of fish littering the wooden planks. The smell of saltwater became more pronounced, adding to the tapestry of sensory details that would forever be imprinted in his memory—a photographic memory.

Behind him, the SUV had stopped. Doors slammed as two men got out, watching after him. He didn't focus on them, and instead, his eyes locked onto the sleek speedboat bobbing gently at the dock.

His bodyguards watched from afar, poised to leap into action the moment their employer reached the boat.

As the Architect's foot finally met the worn wooden planks of the wharf, he felt a surge of exhilaration.

"Boss!" one of the bodyguards called out, his hand extended to help the Architect aboard.

With a swift, fluid motion, the Architect leaped onto the deck, not missing a beat. "Go!" he barked, his eyes locked on the receding harbor.

"Roger that," the bodyguard at the helm replied, pushing the throttle forward with practiced ease.

As the boat roared to life, the Architect's mind raced, calculating distances, angles, and escape routes. The challenge of it all was intoxicating. He felt alive.

"Smooth sailing from here, Boss?" one of the bodyguards asked, barely raising his voice above the engine's growl.

"Never assume anything," the Architect replied, his gaze unwavering. "We've got a long way to go before we reach Mr. Porter."

"Understood," the bodyguard said, nodding his head.

"Keep your eyes peeled for any unexpected surprises," he added, more to himself than anyone else. Surprises were something the Architect had learned to anticipate but never welcome.

However, very, very soon, it would be Porter faced with a truly painful surprise.

Suddenly, his phone began chirping. He frowned. Only two people had that number.

He pulled the phone swiftly, sea spray speckling his rigid, unmoving features. "Yes?" he said simply. He paused, listening. "The GPS? Where? You're sure? Pick him up. Yes, I'm sure. *Now.*"

He hung up, frowning.

Two of his guards were watching him curiously.

"Faster!" he snapped. "Go!"

Sometimes, even the best-laid plans...

But no matter. A minor hiccup. The GPS was heading in the wrong direction. The team that had taken out the meddling witness was off course.

But that would be rectified soon enough.

Nothing would stop this now.

He'd been planning it all for so very long.

Chapter 11

Ella's heart raced, though not just because of Priscilla's reckless driving. She kept her gaze fixed on the rearview mirror, scanning for any signs of danger, her right hand playing absentmindedly with the small, GPS tracking unit she'd kept in her pocket. The same unit she'd lied to Cilla about—she hadn't turned it off.

And now they were the bait.

In the storm, it was nearly impossible to tell if there was anyone—or anything—following them. But she couldn't shake the feeling that they were being watched, hunted.

The biting wind howled like a pack of wolves as it whipped around the black 2019 Chevrolet Suburban. The snowstorm had reduced visibility to mere yards, but that didn't seem to bother Priscilla as she expertly navigated the treacherous mountain road back to Nome. Her eyes were narrowed against the blizzard, her grip on the steering wheel tight and steady. She'd always been the one who thought even the weather could bend to her will.

"Slow down, will you?" Ella said, clutching the door handle so tightly her knuckles turned white. There was a growing chasm between her and her twin sister, evident in every sullen silence that stretched between their seats.

"Relax, sis," Priscilla replied, a sardonic grin forming on her lips. "I've driven in worse conditions than this."

"Have you ever considered that maybe I don't want to die today?" Ella asked, trying to keep her voice steady. She found cracks in her calm facade, now. Her anxiety mounting every time she glanced in the rearview mirror which only revealed snow-streaked, desolate highway behind them.

Cilla, sensing the nerves in her sister, just smiled sweetly. Or perhaps it was more like the leer of a hyena before it moved in for the kill.

"Come on, Ella. You're the one with all the dangerous hobbies," Priscilla retorted, swerving left and then right as if testing the limits of the SUV. "Besides, we're almost there."

Ella bit her lip, her thoughts racing. If only Priscilla knew what she had gotten herself into. She couldn't afford to let her emotions cloud her judgment. There was too much at stake.

"Priscilla, I need you to listen to me," Ella said, her voice shaking slightly. "There's something you should know."

"Is this another one of your FBI secrets?" Priscilla asked, the bitterness in her voice cutting through the howling wind.

"Just... just be careful, please," Ella pleaded. But her words fell on deaf ears, her sister too focused on maneuvering the vehicle through the storm.

"Trust goes both ways, Ella," Priscilla spat out, swerving the SUV again, narrowly avoiding a snowbank. "You want me to trust you? Start by trusting me."

Ella swallowed hard, her eyes still glued to the rearview mirror.

Ella's hand slid into the pocket of her jacket, fingers brushing against the cold metal of the GPS tracker. The small, black, rectangular device blinked with a red light that seemed to pulse in time with her own heartbeat. She pulled it out, careful not to let Priscilla notice, and stared at it for a moment, her heart pounding in her chest.

"Shit," she mouthed.

"Did you say something?" Priscilla asked, eyes darting over to Ella.

"Nothing," Ella replied quickly, slipping the GPS tracker back into her pocket. She'd taken it from the dead gunman an hour before, hoping it would lead them straight to his accomplices and, ultimately, their boss. But the plan meant putting themselves in danger.

"Priscilla," she began, trying to find the right words. "I... I need to tell you something."

"Oh? And what's that?" Priscilla replied, her gaze focused on the road ahead, the snowstorm swallowing up the world around them. And yet, even now, Cilla managed a hint of sarcasm in her voice.

Ella hesitated then added, "You know the GPS tracker from the gunman? I lied. It's not off. It's active, and I kept it in my pocket."

Priscilla's eyes widened, her grip tightening on the steering wheel. "Why would you keep it on us? Are you insane?"

"Because if they come after us," Ella took a deep breath, "we can take one alive and make him lead us back to their boss."

"You're... insane," Cilla said, scowling. "Why didn't you just *tell* me?"

Ella hesitated. She'd been wondering this herself. Because she didn't trust her sister? But how did she say something like that aloud?

Because it was too important?

Or just... *because.* A sister thing.

She grimaced, wishing it was Brenner in the car instead of Cilla.

"Priscilla, I didn't—" Ella began, but her sister cut her off.

"Save it," Priscilla snapped. "We're doing it your way, as always. Let's just hope your plan doesn't get us both killed."

Ella clenched her jaw, her eyes darting back to the rearview mirror. She couldn't let her fear control her now. She had to be strong for both of them. As the SUV raced through the storm, she thought of all the lives that would be saved if they could put an end to this madness—and all the lives that would be lost if they failed.

The tension between the sisters hung heavy in the air, like a thick fog. It was a palpable presence, an unspoken war of wills. Priscilla glanced at her sister, trying to read her thoughts. "What are you looking for?" she asked.

"Nothing," Ella replied curtly, her eyes fixed on the rearview mirror. She couldn't afford any distractions. Not when they were so close to putting an end to this nightmare.

"Clearly it's not nothing," Priscilla retorted, her voice sharp as a knife. "You've been staring into that mirror for the past fifteen minutes. Are you expecting company? You think they're going to come at us *here*? On the move?"

"I don't know. Can we just focus on getting back to Nome?" Ella shot back, her face a mask of determination. But beneath her steely exterior, a storm of doubt raged.

"Typical... No wonder he likes you."

Ella tensed, glancing sharply at her sister.

Priscilla seemed to be waiting, like a fisherman at the end of a reel, watching a fish nibble.

Ella didn't say anything, but she knew better than to expect her sister to just let it go.

Priscilla said, "Brenner dated me as a substitute, you know. We did more than date." Her hands were gripping the steering wheel tightly.

Ella could feel her lips pressing in a thin line.

"Let's just drop it," Ella said.

"Why would I drop something I picked up to begin with? Hmm? Though you seem to like my sloppy seconds, don't you."

Ella looked at her sister, her eyes flashing.

This elicited a grin from Priscilla. "Ah, there it is. Hidden behind those pretty curtains. But it's there. Are you upset, sis?"

Ella kept her mouth sealed. It was a matter of principle for her not to rise to someone's taunting. She'd sat in the front of cars while serial killers in the back had uttered all sorts of horrific obscenities and threats... and she hadn't batted an eye.

But Cilla had a way of getting under her skin.

"He liked being with me more, though," Cilla said in a sort of sing-song voice, still gripping the steering wheel as if she were trying to strangle it. "You never did put out back then, did you? Have you gotten a bit more frisky in your old age, sis? Got a favorite position now?"

"Cilla, cut it out. I mean it."

"Or what? Hmm? Gonna go running to Brenny-poo?"

Ella had never wanted to hit someone so badly before.

But even as she felt her fist clenching, she was distracted by a blur behind them.

Before either sister could say another word, the sudden, high-pitched whine of engines cut through the air, jolting them both back to the moment. Ella's simmering anger quickly turned to horror.

Her heart raced as she peered into the rearview mirror once more, her breath catching in her throat as she spotted three snowmobiles racing towards them, closing the gap at an alarming speed.

"Shit, watch out!" Ella exclaimed, pointing ahead. A large, toppled truck blocked the road, a white semi-trailer with the word Arctic painted in blue letters lay on its side, creating an impassable barrier.

"Damn it!" Priscilla cursed under her breath, her eyes darting between the approaching snowmobiles and the wrecked truck.

"Get ready," Ella warned, gripping her Glock tightly.

"Damn it, Ella!" Priscilla snarled, her anger flaring. Priscilla expertly swerved the black SUV to the right, narrowly avoiding the toppled semi-trailer, but the gap was tight, and sparks exploded off the side of their vehicle as they scraped on a concrete barrier. But they managed to avoid a collision.

With a sharp jerk to the left, she steered them back onto the empty highway, only to veer right again as the first bullets from the snowmobiles peppered the side of their vehicle.

"Stay focused," Ella snapped, her voice cold and controlled despite the chaos unfolding around them. She couldn't afford to let her emotions get the better of her—not now.

"Focus?!" Priscilla shouted incredulously. "You're insane! Truly!"

Clenching her jaw, Ella raised her Glock 19, the black handgun fitted with a laser sight. She took aim at the nearest snowmobile, the red dot dancing across the driver's chest before she squeezed the trigger.

The sound of gunshots mingled with the howling wind and the crunch of tires on snow, creating a cacophony that resonated deep in Ella's bones. The snowflakes that swirled around them seemed almost surreal in contrast to the violence that surrounded the sisters.

"Keep driving—I'll handle this," Ella ordered, her eyes fixed on the snowmobiles as she fired off another round. One of the attackers, who'd been aiming a pistol towards the driver-side window of their SUV, slumped over his handlebars.

"Fine," Priscilla muttered, her eyes narrowed in determination as she continued her evasive maneuvers.

"We got this," Ella murmured, more to herself than her sister, as she fired another shot at the remaining snowmobiles.

The SUV fishtailed dangerously across the icy highway, tires screeching in protest as Priscilla struggled to keep control. Ella held on tight, her knuckles white and her heart pounding as she leaned out the window to fire another shot. The windshield wipers worked furiously to clear their view, but it was a losing battle against the relentless snowfall.

Ella shouted over the roar of the wind, frustration etched on her face. "Can't you keep this thing steady?"

"Kinda hard when we're being chased by armed lunatics!" Priscilla snapped back, her voice strained under the stress of the situation. She clenched her jaw and focused her attention on the road ahead.

Ella gritted her teeth and ignored the sting of the cold wind on her face as she took aim at one of the snowmobiles. A well-placed shot hit the rider squarely in the chest, causing him to tumble off his vehicle, leaving a crimson stain on the pristine white snow. The remaining snowmobile revved its engine, undeterred and hell-bent on catching up to the sisters.

"One more to go," Ella muttered under her breath, her steely gaze locked on her final target.

But then, horrified, she realized the first snowmobiler had recovered. He was trying to sneak up at their flank.

She moved, aimed. With practiced precision, she fired again, this time hitting the engine of the second snowmobile. It sputtered and died, the rider cursing loudly as he veered off the road and disappeared from sight.

"Brace yourself, Cilla!" Ella warned, quickly assessing the situation. "I'll cover you—just ram that last one!"

"Are you insane?" Priscilla yelled, her eyes wide with disbelief. But even as she questioned her sister's plan, she tightened her grip on the wheel and steered toward the remaining snowmobile.

Ella shouted, her voice desperate and pleading. "We have to take one alive. Think about dad!"

Silently cursing her sister's stubbornness, Priscilla accelerated. The snowmobile rider seemed to realize what was about to happen and tried to swerve out of the way, but it was too late. With a sickening crunch of metal on metal, the SUV slammed into the vehicle, pinning it against the highway barrier.

The car jolted, both sisters lurching forward.

"Did we get him?" Priscilla asked between labored breaths, her hands still gripping the steering wheel as if her life depended on it.

"Looks like it," Ella replied, her voice hollow. But she was already moving.

With the third snowmobile crushed against the barrier, Ella and Priscilla sprang from the SUV, guns drawn. Snowflakes clung to their eyelashes as they moved with purpose.

"Hands where I can see them!" Ella barked at the man in the black ski mask, her voice sharp against the howling wind. The attacker lay pinned under his wrecked vehicle, but he managed to lift his hands in surrender.

"Help me get him out," Ella told Priscilla, her eyes never leaving the gunman. Priscilla nodded, holstering her weapon and working quickly to free the man from the twisted mess of metal.

"Got him," she grunted, yanking the assailant free and shoving him toward Ella. The sisters exchanged a quick glance, silently acknowledging the danger they were still in. They needed answers, and fast.

"Get in the car," Ella ordered, pushing their captive towards the open door. He stumbled, his breaths coming in ragged gasps beneath his mask. Priscilla slid back behind the wheel, her eyes flickering between the rearview mirror and her sister.

"Start talking," Ella demanded, her gun unwavering as she stared at the man now handcuffed in their backseat. He said nothing, his eyes darting between the sisters, taking in every detail. Ella's heart pounded in her chest, adrenaline coursing through her veins, but she maintained her composure—the man was their only lead to the mastermind behind this attack.

She slammed the door shut, the sound echoing through the snowy landscape like the crack of a gunshot.

"Let's get out of here," Ella said, her gaze meeting Priscilla's in the rearview mirror. Her sister nodded silently and floored the accelerator, leaving the wreckage and the abandoned snowmobiles behind them, their engines sputtering out as the storm swallowed them whole.

Ella quickly called paramedics, though, there was little hope for the two snowmobilers she'd hit center mass.

"Who are these people?" Priscilla asked, unable to keep the frustration from her voice. She gripped the wheel harder, focusing on the treacherous road ahead. Ella stared at the silent man in the backseat, her mind racing with possibilities.

"I don't know yet," she admitted, her voice laced with uncertainty. "But we're going to find out."

The sisters sped through the blizzard, their SUV a lone beacon of light amidst the swirling darkness. The handcuffed man remained silent, his eyes darting between the two women.

There was something distinctly unnerving about his gaze.

No fear. No agitation.

Just... curiosity, as if he were examining two specimens under a microscope.

Ella hesitated for a brief moment, her mind moving back to Mortimer Graves, and then she shouted. "Wait! Pull over!"

"What?"

"I said pull over!"

It was against Priscilla's core values to do *anything* Ella suggested, but the shock of the moment seemed to distract her from this childhood vow and she pulled slowly to the side of the road, leaving gouges in the snowy ground cover.

Ella swallowed once, steeled herself, and then, eyes narrowed, she flung open the door, slipping out into the blizzard, her jaw set in determination.

Chapter 12

Ella grabbed the man by the collar, pulling him out into the snow. She flung him to the ground, pointing her weapon at him.

He smirked up at her. Without his ski mask, he looked like a choir boy gone bad. Neatly parted hair held in place by a helmet of product, but a scar traced over his eyebrow. He had a small mustache that was closer to peach fuzz than facial hair, but his jaw was pronounced.

He could've been either twenty or forty.

This seemed a commonality to the men she'd been encountering involved in all of this. They were the sorts that had... *unusual* features.

Now, though, standing over him in the snow, gun trained on his head, she said, "Don't move."

He looked up at her, his breath fogging the eye, his nostrils flaring with each rapid breath. "You think you scare me?" he whispered.

She didn't say anything.

"You don't scare me." He spoke with a faintly Eastern European accent. "You don't know fear."

His lips twisted back like bread dough. "I say nothing. You do nothing." His accent had become more pronounced as he glared at her.

Ella studied him for a moment. "I don't expect you to sell him out. The Architect, I mean. But that's fine."

She gave him a hollow little smile. "I'm not interested in your cooperation. Just your phone."

She reached into his pocket as he tried to avoid her hand, and she withdrew his phone.

The cold wind whipped around them. And the man was shivering now where he sat in a snow drift on the side of the road.

Ella raised the phone, frowning at it. She slid her finger along the screen and then returned his smirk. She clucked her tongue. "Aww... no password protection? Big bad boss likes things out in the open, I bet. Most control freaks do."

He was glaring at her now as she cycled through his phone. She raised it, using it to place a call to a forensic tech she knew back in Seattle.

Guyves had a phone she'd sent him months ago but hadn't been able to crack it yet. Part of her wondered if it was a lack of ability... or willingness.

Now, though, as her call connected, a voice answered on the other end.

"Porter?"

"Guyves."

"Wassup, girl?"

Ella held back a smile at the familiar voice. "This number. Can you locate its GPS history?"

"Mhmm."

"You can?"

"Just did."

"What... like now?"

"Mhmm. New software, baby cakes. Built it ground up myself. Silicon Valley here I come."

Ella raised an eyebrow but kept her tone in check. "Can you send me a report of the last known location for that phone? Going back two weeks."

"Can't do. New phone. Only been live three days."

Ella frowned, but then she hesitated. Three days... the governor was killed in that window. They still hadn't found the governor's body.

She said, softly, "Where was the last location five hours ago?"

"Five? Hmm... Oh shit."

"What?"

"Spotty. Means it was underground."

Ella tensed. "Where?"

"Ever heard of the Permafrost Tunnel? That research one?"

"Yeah."

"He was there, doll. About ten hours ago. Left five ago."

That was right after the governor had been killed.

"Thanks, Guyves. And... any luck on that phone I sent you?"

"Nah. Not yet. I think it's wiped. But I'll keep you posted."

Ella frowned, lowering the phone.

"The Permafrost Tunnel?" she said, glancing at the man sitting in the snowbank.

As the snow flurried around them, and both of them shivered, she could tell he'd tensed.

She nodded once. "Thanks."

And then she turned, moving back to the car.

"Wait! Hey—hey, lady! You can't leave me here."

She looked back at him. "I wasn't going to. Though, if you were involved in torturing that witness... I can't say you'd deserve better."

She opened the door, watching as he stumbled towards the car, shivering.

And then she pushed him in, slammed the door, and placed a call.

"Brenner?" she said. "Yeah... Yeah, I'm fine. I need you to check something for me. Call it in, please. Yeah, I'm heading back. You, too."

She hurried around the side of the SUV.

The killer had been in the Permafrost Tunnel. And the video of the governor looked as if it had been taken underground.

Would they discover his body there?

She trembled slightly at the thought... Part of her felt as if she already knew the answer.

Chapter 13

The snowflakes danced in the frigid Alaskan air as Ella surveyed the scene before her. Her breath came out in frosty puffs, mingling with the winter breeze.

"Think they found the body?" Cilla said sarcastically.

The sound of the helicopter Chief Baker had chartered for them was still whirring behind them where it had deposited them outside the landing pad of the Permafrost Research Tunnel.

The reason for Cilla's sarcastic comment was the horde of emergency responders now traipsing over the tunnel entrance, streaming in and out like ants.

Ella had never seen so many flashing lights and uniforms. She spotted where a couple of cops were using a digger to clear snow away to allow an off-terrain truck to approach up the side of a hill.

"I'm guessing yes," Ella said with a grimace.

She scanned the gathered responders, looking for Brenner.

The sunlight beat down on them, blindingly oppressive after the multi-hour wait and flight through treacherous winds.

The US Marshal was supposed to meet them here. Ella wondered if he was staying out of sight until Priscilla disappeared.

Cilla didn't wait to confer. Instead, she broke into an urgent stride with the gait of someone twice her height.

She marched in the direction of the looming tunnel entrance ahead, an ominous gash carved into the frozen earth, framed by jagged icicles that seemed to reach for them like the fingers of some malevolent force.

As Ella approached the tunnel, she couldn't help but shudder at the thought of what lay within. The darkness seemed to swallow her up as she stepped inside, the cold seeping into her bones. A faint, eerie glow emanated from the walls, cast by the chemical lights that had been placed to illuminate the crime scene. The permeating scent of damp earth and decay lingered in the air, a stark reminder of the grim task at hand.

The tunnel stretched out before them, seemingly endless, with jagged icicles hanging from the ceiling like menacing stalactites. The air was frigid and dense, carrying an unmistakable earthy scent that mingled with the icy chill.

As she ventured deeper, Ella noticed the subtle shift in temperature, the biting cold intensifying with each step. The walls, hewn from ancient ice and frozen soil, appeared almost ethereal, their translucent layers holding stories untold for thousands of years. Thin layers of frost glistened like delicate lace, as if nature herself had draped the tunnel in an ethereal garment.

The agent's breath escaped in visible puffs, adding to the mysterious atmosphere that enveloped her. The rhythmic drip of melting ice echoed through the silent corridor, amplifying the eerie solitude. Whispers seemed to emanate from the frozen walls.

Occasionally, Ella's flashlight would illuminate pockets of frozen artifacts, suspended in time. Ancient bones of small, prehistoric animals lay embedded in the permafrost, their well-preserved forms silently testifying to an era long gone.

"God, it's like stepping into another world," Priscilla whispered, her breath hitching as they ventured deeper into the tunnel.

"Stay focused," Ella reminded her sister, trying to shake off her own creeping unease.

Together, the two sisters pressed onward, their strained relationship momentarily eclipsed by the urgency of their mission. As they delved deeper into the icy labyrinth, the haunting echoes of their footsteps seemed to reverberate through the very walls, driving home the chilling reality of what had transpired within this frozen tomb. A man with a camera around his neck stepped aside as Ella flashed her badge, allowing them to pass. Two women who were trying to move a gurney paused, frowning as one wiped sweat from her brow.

Upon reaching the heart of the Permafrost Tunnel, Ella and Priscilla were met with a grisly tableau. A flurry of activity surrounded the crime scene, with local law enforcement officers and forensic experts carefully documenting every detail. The air was thick with tension, each person acutely aware of their role in uncovering the truth behind this heinous act.

"Shit," Cilla muttered under her breath as she caught sight of the governor's lifeless body. He was bound to a rickety wooden chair, wrists secured with coarse rope that bit into his pale flesh. His right hand was left free, an unnerving image given the gun that lay ominously at his side.

"Disturbing, isn't it?" Ella said quietly, taking in the grim scene before them. "It's almost like they wanted him to have a fighting chance."

"Or they wanted to make it look like he had one," Priscilla countered, her eyes narrowing as she considered the implications. "Did you watch the video?"

"Yeah."

"Someone was commanding him off-screen. Not a suicide at all."

"Definitely not," Ella agreed, her gaze locked on the governor's face. She could feel her pulse quicken, the familiar thrill of the hunt coursing through her veins. This was where she excelled, unraveling the threads of seemingly unsolvable mysteries.

"Ms. Porter," called one of the officers, clearly recognizing at least one of the twins. "And... Agent Porter, I presume?"

"Eleanor," Priscilla supplied with a tight smile.

But before her sister could take control of the conversation, Ella asked, "Is there something we should know about the crime scene?"

"Actually, yes," the officer replied, gesturing towards the tunnel walls. "We found traces of blood splatter near the entrance. It doesn't match the governor's blood type, so there might be another victim or perpetrator out there."

"Interesting," Ella mused, her mind already working through the possibilities. "Anything else?"

"We're still processing the scene," the officer admitted. "But it's slow going, with the cold and all."

"Understood," Ella said, nodding solemnly. "We'll take a look around, see if anything jumps out at us."

As they moved further into the tunnel, Ella couldn't shake the feeling that they were being watched. It was as if the very walls held secrets, whispering malevolent promises to those who dared to listen.

Ella crouched down beside the governor's body, her breath misting in the cold air as she examined the scene with a meticulous eye. She took note of the gun lying next to his hand, the way his fingers were still curled around it ever so slightly. Priscilla watched from the sidelines, her arms folded tightly across her chest as she let Ella work.

"Something's off," Ella muttered under her breath, her gaze locked on the governor's face. His expression was twisted in pain, but that wasn't what had caught her attention.

"Like what?" Priscilla asked, stepping closer.

"His tooth... he's missing one," Ella said, pointing to the gap in the governor's teeth. "It looks like it's been pulled out recently. Same as Margaret."

"Maybe it happened during a struggle?" Priscilla suggested, furrowing her brow.

"Could be," Ella agreed, standing up and approaching the coroner, who was busy taking photographs of the scene. "Excuse me, Dr. Shaw? I noticed that the governor is missing a tooth. Any thoughts on that?"

Dr. Shaw lowered his camera and turned to Ella, his glasses fogging up slightly in the cold. "Ah, yes. Er, agent..."

"Porter."

"Right... right. We've noticed that as well. It appears to have been extracted forcibly, but there's no sign of the tooth in the immediate vicinity. We'll be conducting a more thorough search, of course."

"Thank you, Doctor," Ella replied, nodding her appreciation. She glanced back at the governor's body, her mind racing through various scenarios, each darker than the last.

Why would someone pull out his tooth? Was it some sort of sick message? Or perhaps a trophy?

"Hey, Ella?" Priscilla called out, snapping her sister out of her thoughts. "I think I found something over here."

Ella hurried over to where Priscilla was standing, her boots crunching on the frozen ground. As she joined her sister, she saw a small, metal object partially buried in the dirt.

"Looks like some kind of tool," Ella observed, carefully extracting the item with gloved hands. "But it's not something I recognize."

"Could be related to the missing tooth?" Priscilla suggested, her eyes narrowing as she examined the object.

"Maybe," Ella agreed, placing the tool into an evidence bag and sealing it shut. The tool was hooked, like a dentist's probe. "We'll have to get it analyzed."

But then Dr. Shaw winced. "Ah, er, ladies. Sorry. That's mine. I was looking for it." He hurried over, snatching the instrument and shaking his head apologetically as he skittered off again.

Ella frowned after him, shook her head, and said, "Hang on, could we—"

But he didn't look back. She wanted to go after him but then thought better of it, and returned her attention to the tunnel's floor. Did she really think the *coroner* was somehow involved? She shook her head in irritation.

As they continued to search for clues, Ella's mind refused to quiet down.

Ella and Priscilla, their breaths clouding in the frigid tunnel air, moved deeper into the permafrost cavern. The low hum of the generator powering the crime scene lights bounced off the icy walls, creating an eerie atmosphere that seemed to cling to them like a second skin.

"Check out these scrapes on the wall," Cilla pointed out, her gloved finger tracing the jagged lines etched into the ice. "What do you make of them?"

"Could be from tools used to maintain the tunnels, or something dragged along the walls," Ella mused, her mind racing with possibilities. She snapped a few photos for future reference before continuing their search.

With every step they took, their boots crunched against the frozen ground, while droplets of water fell from the icicles above like a discordant symphony.

"Hey, look at this," Priscilla said, crouching down near a patch of disturbed dirt. Ella joined her sister, her gaze drawn to the odd markings left behind.

"Tripod legs," Ella murmured, her eyes narrowing as she inspected the pattern. "Someone filmed the governor's death. This must be where they recorded it."

"Pretty sick, huh?" Priscilla replied, her voice strained. "Using your own victim as the star of your twisted show."

"Let's get some casts made of these marks," Ella directed, her determination flaring. "And I want to know everything about this tripod—material, brand, where it can be purchased."

As the forensic team got to work, Ella took a closer look at the markings on the ground.

Cilla, though, was saying, "Bit big for a normal tripod. The legs would be made of lightweight carbon fiber, each one extending telescopically and ending in sharp spikes."

"Spikes?"

"Yup. Alaska," Cilla said by way of explanation. "Have to use them when gauging new dig sites."

"Anything else?" Ella glanced at her sister, surprised to find Cilla useful for a change.

Priscilla shrugged. "Probably was designed for use in rugged environments, with adjustable leg angles and a compact, foldable frame for easy transportation. I mean... they got it down here, didn't they?"

"Any idea what sort of model it might be?" Ella asked.

"Nah. But they should be able to figure it out," Cilla said, nodding towards the techs now leaning down to take a 3D, optical mold with their phones.

Ella watched, frowning.

It was a tenuous lead.

Marks in the dirt.

A missing tooth. A dead governor.

What did any of it mean?

She frowned, turning once more towards the governor's body. She noticed something else, now, standing there.

His shoelaces were missing.

Ella began to speak when a voice called out behind them. "Ella?"

She turned, glancing back towards a blue-eyed, handsome man striding towards them. He had some scruff, and a scar was visible past his collar. His frame was lanky and lean, and the windbreaker he wore hardly seemed sufficient given the climate. He strode hurriedly towards her, a look of concern across his features.

Before Ella could call out, though, Priscilla frowned, turned, and swung her fist as hard as she could, aiming for the man's jaw.

Chapter 14

Ella watched in horror as Priscilla's fist connected with Brenner's jaw, and he reeled back. Her sister lunged at her boyfriend and shoved him hard, sending him tumbling over an old electric generator with a grunt.

He hit the ground but bounced up quick.

For a brief moment, Brenner stretched to his full height, his chest puffing out, his arms like iron cords at his sides.

He glared at Cilla, his eyes blazing.

In that brief instance, Ella realized that Brenner Gunn was more than she usually saw.

As an ex-Navy SEAL, who'd been known as the guardian angel to his team, Brenner had a killer's past. He was the best marksman she'd ever seen, and though he walked with a limp on his right leg from an old injury, he was also one of the toughest men she'd ever known.

But dangerous too.

And now, staring at him, she realized it was all in the eyes.

Still, he was restrained. He didn't lash out. Didn't say much. He kept his hands locked into fists at his side but never moved an inch towards Priscilla.

"Whoopsie," Cilla said, smiling at him. She massaged her knuckles. "Sorry. I tripped."

A couple of cops instinctively turned to face the scuffle, only to hurriedly turn away when they saw who it was. Even out here, the Princess of Nome would continue to enjoy her royal privilege, it seemed.

Brenner, meanwhile, was breathing deeply—in, out, breathing through his nose.

"What the hell?" he said at last, his jaw clenched. The angry, red marks from Cilla's punch were visible against his skin.

Cilla leaned back, reclining against a permafrost wall as if she were a cat lounging in the sun. "How's it goin' Brens?" she said conversationally, as if nothing had just happened.

Brenner allowed a growl into his throat. "What. The. Hell," he said again.

"Told you. Whoops."

Ella scowled at her sister, turning to face her. Sometimes, keeping her emotions in check, her face impassive, it helped to defuse situations.

But other times, it was a disloyalty. Brenner had been struck, and she was just standing there.

She felt her own temper flare, and her expression curdled into a scowl.

The frigid air of the Permafrost Tunnel nipped at Ella Porter's cheeks as she shivered, standing, facing her twin. The dim lighting cast eerie shadows on the walls, creating a somber atmosphere. It was a stark contrast to the flurry of activity from the crime scene techs and agents swarming around them, their movements precise and methodical. But it was as if the altercation was invisible—as if the other LEOs hadn't seen a thing.

Ella frowned at Priscilla, whose eyes were alight with a mixture of anger and determination. She knew that look; it was one that had often preceded heated arguments in their childhood. Her breath hitched.

"Pris," Ella started, trying to keep her voice steady, "I know you're upset, but lashing out won't help."

"Upset?" Priscilla scoffed, her voice like ice. "You have no idea."

Without warning, Priscilla tried to strike Brenner again, swinging her fist. The force behind the punch was so raw, so primal, that it seemed to temporarily silence the commotion around them. But Brenner saw it coming this time and stepped quickly back, avoiding the blow.

"Priscilla!" Ella cried, reaching out and catching her sister's shoulder in an attempt to calm her down. She could feel the tension in every muscle beneath her fingers. "Stop!"

Priscilla glanced down at Ella's fingers, and that same rage smoldered in her gaze. "Let. Me. Go."

Ella's mind raced, trying to find the right words to diffuse the situation. She knew her sister too well; once Priscilla had made up her mind about something, there was little that could convince her otherwise.

And yet, she couldn't just stand idly by as her twin attacked the man she loved.

"Pris, please," Ella said firmly, her grip on her sister's shoulder tightening. "We can talk through whatever it is that's bothering you."

Priscilla shrugged off Ella's touch as if it burned her, taking a menacing step towards Brenner. Her eyes were wild and bloodshot, filled with years of hurt and betrayal.

"You think this is just going to work out, huh?" she spat at him, her voice trembling with barely contained fury. The crime scene techs and agents glanced over with discomfort, trying to focus on their work and avoid the escalating confrontation.

"What's going to work out?" Ella asked, her heart pounding in her chest as she tried to make sense of her sister's accusations. She knew that Priscilla had always been fiercely protective of her family, but this level of anger was something else entirely. She was clearly concerned about their father, clearly scared. Seeing what had happened to the governor, likely made her think the same would happen to her father. But the anger in Cilla's gaze went even deeper than that.

"He likes blondes, hmm," Cilla said. She glanced at her sister. "Carpet match the drapes? I don't have carpet. You know what I mean?"

She spoke loud, completely indifferent to the figures around them, watching.

"Enough!" Ella interjected. "The past is the past, Pris. We can't change what happened, and neither of us want to see anyone get hurt."

"Speak for yourself," Priscilla muttered darkly, her gaze never leaving Brenner.

Ella's mind raced as she tried to come up with a way to defuse the situation.

Ella looked back and forth between her twin and Brenner. The tension in the air was so thick that it felt almost suffocating.

"Face it, Ella," Priscilla spat, her eyes narrowing. "You stole Brenner from me and ruined my life."

Ella's heart clenched at the accusation, but she was also taken aback. *Ruined*? Where was this coming from? She took a deep breath, her gaze flicking between Priscilla and Brenner, who was standing stiffly, his expression unreadable.

"Stole him?" Ella's voice was incredulous. "Is that really what you think?"

For a moment, it was as if *both* sisters forgot anyone else was watching. They both glared at each other.

Ella felt like she was fifteen again. Her jaw clenched, and her eyes narrowed. Unspoken accusations burbled up, and she said, in a seething voice, "You tried to steal him from me."

"Psh. You left."

"Because my family was full of assholes," Ella retorted.

Cilla smirked, but there was no humor in her eyes. "Is that the best you've got? Come on, Agent Porter. Tell me how you really feel?"

"Yeah? Should I? I am an agent... but what are you?"

"And what does that mean?"

Ella felt like an alcoholic finally giving in. She tempered herself on cussing, yelling, rage... But now... she let it loose. She could feel her face reddening, could feel eyes darting towards her. This was a damn crime scene, after all, but it didn't matter.

"You made your choices, Pris. You chose to get involved in all those shady moves with the gold mine. And don't even get me started on Dad's business dealings."

Priscilla's face contorted with rage, the mention of their father cutting deep. "You have no idea what it was like trying to survive after you left!" she snarled. "I had to do whatever it took to keep going!"

"By exploiting people?" Ella countered, anger rising within her. "By stepping on anyone who got in your way?"

The crime scene techs and agents seemed to hold their breath collectively, trying to give the sisters space while still attending to their duties. The oppressive weight of the ice-covered walls seemed to close in on them as the argument escalated.

"Enough!" Priscilla shouted, her face twisted with fury. Before Ella could react, her twin lunged at her, fingers clawing for purchase on her throat.

Brenner moved quickly, grabbing Priscilla's wrist just as her hand was about to wrap around Ella's neck. His grip was firm, yet gentle, as he held her back. The sudden intervention only served to enrage Priscilla further, and she struggled against his restraining hold, her face flushed with fury.

"Let go of me!" she screamed, her voice echoing through the tunnel.

Ella felt her own anger warring with concern for Brenner. What would he think of her now? Now that he'd seen her like this? Completely out of control, just like Cilla. Priscilla had always been impulsive, but this was something else entirely. She searched for words that could possibly reach through the maelstrom of emotions and bring her twin back from the brink.

"Pris, please," she whispered, her voice trembling.

Her sister's eyes locked onto hers, a storm of pain and bitterness swirling within them. In that moment, Ella knew with a sinking feeling that there might be no going back for either of them.

The silence that followed was deafening. Brenner's chest rose and fell with his ragged breathing, but he remained rooted in place, his hand still wrapped around Priscilla's wrist as though afraid to let go. Ella could see the resignation etched onto his face, a quiet sadness that seemed to age him before her eyes.

"Can't you see what you're doing?" Ella asked Priscilla, her voice barely audible. "We're family."

"We've never been family!"

"I know... That wasn't my choice. You chose gold over blood!"

"Gold?! You think this is about gold?" Priscilla spat out, her glare never leaving Ella's face. She tried to wrench her arm free from Brenner's grip, but he held on, keeping her at bay. "This is about betrayal, Ella. Betrayal by the one person I thought would always have my back."

"Pris..." Ella whispered, the word heavy with sorrow. But even as she reached out for her sister, she knew her touch would not be welcomed. Instead, she clenched her fist, feeling the cold air bite into her skin as her heart ached.

Brenner's eyes flickered between them, an unspoken plea for peace. Faced with the storm of emotions threatening to tear them apart, he seemed unsure of how to proceed.

"Please," he finally said, the word like a prayer. "Cilla, just stop."

"Stop?" Priscilla sneered, her anger unabated. "You want me to stop? Fine. Let's all pretend everything's fine and dandy while you play house with my twin sister and forget about our child. Our history."

"I've suffered too," he said simply. His tone was rock solid, but his eyes held the same pain mirrored in Cilla's.

"Priscilla, we've talked about this," Ella interjected, desperation creeping into her voice. "We can't keep rehashing the past. We have to move forward."

"Move forward?" Priscilla laughed bitterly, her eyes glistening with unshed tears. "That's rich, coming from the woman who stole my future."

Ella flinched as though struck. The words cut deep but she also knew that they couldn't change what had happened; they could only try to heal the wounds left behind.

"Pris, I'm sorry," Ella said quietly, her voice thick with emotion. "I shouldn't have left. I know that now."

For a moment, it seemed as though Priscilla might relent—that the fire in her eyes might dim, and the sister Ella had known and loved as a young girl might emerge from the ashes. But then, with a snarl of frustration, she ripped her arm free from Brenner's grasp, stumbling back as she glared at them both.

"Fine," she spat. "Have it your way. But don't expect me to stick around and watch. You don't wanna help Dad. I'll go do something about it."

And with that, she turned on her heel and stormed off down the tunnel, leaving Ella and Brenner standing amidst the shattered remains of their family, the icy walls seeming to close in around them as the weight of their choices settled heavily upon their shoulders.

And all the while, a corpse watched them from the corner, those dead eyes staring... staring... *staring*.

Ella shivered, shaking her head. "Shit," she muttered under her breath. She shot a panicked glance at Brenner and winced.

She shook her head, too ashamed to meet his gaze, and began moving off, away down the tunnel as well, in the opposite direction from her sister.

She picked up her pace, moving fast, feeling hot embarrassment course down her spine in prickles.

"Shit... *shit*," she muttered under her breath.

Hardly professional. Hardly stubborn with a smile as she was so often called.

No... she'd just been like her father.

She'd lost it.

She could feel herself hyperventilating, moving quickly away.

After only a few seconds, a hand caught hers. Rough, calloused fingers against her own palm.

She glanced down, then up.

Brenner was walking at her side, holding her hand.

"I'm sorry," she whispered, looking away again, too ashamed to hold his gaze.

"Sorry?" he said. "For what?"

"For... for losing it."

They moved further down the old tunnel, past the thick walls of ice and mud and stone. Ancient walls with ancient debris.

Brenner was shaking his head. "That was the sexiest you've ever been," he said.

She glanced at him, quirking an eyebrow.

"Er, sorry. Wrong word? Coolest? Nicest... Shit, I don't do words, Ella."

They were now far enough down the curving tunnel and out of sight from the crime scene. She faced him now.

"I... I didn't mean to..."

He just held her hand, studying her. "Thanks for defending me," he said quietly.

She nodded, feeling her sorrow ease a fraction.

Brenner squeezed her hand.

"We'll get through this, Ella. I promise."

She smiled, finally meeting his gaze with resolve.

"I know," she said.

And with those words, she felt her heart heal a little. The ache she'd been carrying for so long seemed to lessen slightly, and she felt a glimmer of peace.

Brenner leaned in, wrapping his arms around her. "Thanks for telling the truth."

"W-what? Oh... yeah. I guess."

"But actually... it was sexy."

She smirked into his shoulder, feeling tears slip down her nose. He held her, and she felt his warmth in the cold tunnel.

"We have to go back to Nome," she murmured at last.

"Why?"

"Because I think Cilla is right. I think Dad's in danger. They'll come for him next."

"Alright. I've got your back."

"I know."

She leaned back and kissed him on the cheek. Wiped the tears from her eyes, feeling a bit less ashamed now that only Brenner could see them, and then she turned on her heel, squaring her shoulders.

She held his hand, leading him back through the scene towards the exit.

She felt like a child, gripping his palm tightly. Like two kids in love traipsing through some adventurous terrain.

She'd always admired her sister's indifference to the opinions of others.

And for a moment, she channeled this same sentiment, holding Brenner and moving fast.

But as she passed the body... As those cold, dead eyes watched her... Ella couldn't help but wonder if her father would be next.

She picked up the pace, just a bit, moving faster towards the helipad.

Chapter 15

They'd moved him twice, and Ella now found herself in the third safehouse in just as many hours.

This new safe house was a sprawling manor nestled deep in the heart of Nome's residential district—standing taller than the vast majority of small, utilitarian homes. It was well past midnight, and the pale moonlight struggled to pierce through the thick canopy of clouds above, casting eerie patterns on the stark ground below. The grand structure was built with dark, weathered stones that seemed to blend seamlessly into its surroundings—a testament to its purpose as a hidden sanctuary for those who sought refuge within its walls.

Ella had patrolled twice now, and as she peered out the window of her father's safe house, she double-checked the sentries.

On this particular night, the house was heavily guarded by a dozen loyal men, each stationed at strategic vantage points around the perimeter. Brenner was also patrolling in a sedan, prowling the streets.

Cilla had been the source of the upgraded security and the safe house moving.

She'd also doubled the pay of the guards. They were paid handsomely for their discretion and unwavering loyalty, especially since the life they were tasked to protect belonged to the king of Nome, the harsh and cold owner of the town's most prosperous gold mines.

Inside the house, Ella was doing her part in ensuring her father's safety. Despite their strained relationship, she could not deny the blood ties that bound them together. Her father was a difficult man to love—his relentless pursuit of wealth and power had hardened him over the years, leaving little room for warmth or affection. But she was his flesh and blood, and she knew it was her duty to stand by him in times of danger.

As Ella moved silently through the dimly lit corridors, her senses heightened, she couldn't help but feel a pang of resentment towards her father. He never showed her any tenderness or understanding, treating her more like an asset to be managed than a daughter to be cherished. Yet here she was, risking her life to protect a man who had always placed his own interests above hers. She shook off these thoughts, knowing that now was not the time to dwell on her own grievances. There was a job to be done, and she was determined to do it well.

Ella's footsteps were barely audible as she patrolled the house, each step calculated and precise. Her keen eyes scanned the shadows, searching for any sign of an intruder. The weight of her Glock in its holster gave her a sense of control. She knew how to handle herself and any threat that might come their way.

The floorboards creaked slightly beneath her feet as she approached the kitchen. A faint glow from the fireplace cast flickering shadows across the room, and there she found her father, hunched over a chessboard. Jameson Porter was engrossed in a game against himself, his cold blue eyes darting between the black and white pieces.

"Father, you should be resting," Ella said quietly, crossing her arms over her chest. The man before her seemed like a stranger, though, he had the same, familiar good looks, like a politician. The same impressive height, and sharp, bony features. He wore an immaculate nightrobe made of silk with gold woven in the hem.

"Rest is for the weak," he murmured without looking up. His long, bony fingers moved a pawn forward, the motion smooth and practiced.

Ella sighed and stepped closer, observing the chessboard with a critical eye. Each piece was meticulously carved, depicting warriors and royals ready for battle. They looked almost lifelike as if they could spring into action at any moment. She admired the craftsmanship but couldn't help feeling a pang of sadness—it seemed her father took more interest in these wooden figures than in his own daughter.

"Solace won't save you from the danger outside," she reminded him, her voice firm but tinged with concern. "You need to take this situation seriously."

"Chess is more than just solace, my dear. It's a reminder," Jameson said, finally meeting her gaze. "Every move we make has consequences. And tonight, we're both playing a high-stakes game. Care to play, Ella?" Jameson asked, his tone mild and unassuming. His expression softened, a rare glimpse of warmth in his otherwise icy eyes that seemed to beckon her closer.

Ella hesitated, caught off guard by the sudden shift in his demeanor. She wanted to maintain her resolve, but there was something undeniably tempting about the offer—a chance, perhaps, to reconnect with the man who had once been her rock. She could see it deep within the lines etched on his face: a flicker of the father she used to know.

"You should be in your room," she said instead, her voice wavering ever so slightly as she tried to suppress her yearning for connection. The fight with Cilla had left her thinking on the helicopter ride. Thinking about her family. About deep regrets. Her brow furrowed, revealing a mix of frustration and concern. "You're putting yourself at risk by staying down here."

"Ah, yes," Jameson replied, his expression darkening again like storm clouds rolling in across his features. "The ever-present threat." He gestured dismissively at the shadows beyond the kitchen as if to say they held no power over him. "But I grow weary of cowering in fear. And besides," he tapped a finger on the board, drawing her attention back to the game, "chess has always had a way of sharpening the mind."

Ella clenched her jaw, torn between her duty to protect her father and her desire to reach out to him. But ultimately, she knew they couldn't afford any distractions. The danger lurking in the shadows was all too real, and it was her responsibility to ensure their safety.

"Please, just go to your room," she insisted, her tone firm and unwavering despite the quiver that danced behind her words. Her eyes locked on his, willing him to understand the gravity of the situation.

"Very well," Jameson said at last, his icy gaze challenging her one final time before he relented. He rose from his chair with a sigh, the creak of old bones echoing in the stillness of the night. "But remember,

Ella," he paused, a ghost of a smile playing on his lips, "every move we make has consequences." He paused, though. Then turned, his robe swirling. "On second thought... Why don't we play for it?" He smirked. Jameson settled back into his seat instead of retreating to his room.

Ella hesitated, her gaze flicking between her father's stony expression and the chessboard before her. Was it wise to indulge him in this game while they were both in danger? Her instincts screamed at her to remain alert, but she couldn't deny the sense of control that came from strategizing on the board—a control that was absent in their current situation.

"Alright," she acquiesced, pulling up a chair opposite him. "One game. But we're keeping our guards up."

"Agreed," Jameson replied, his eyes never leaving hers as he gestured for her to make the first move. She knew he was testing her. It was par for the course where Jameson Porter was concerned.

Ella stared intently at the board, analyzing the positions of the pieces. She didn't know the game as well as her father, but she knew sacrifice.

So she moved.

One move at a time.

She went for a Scholar's Mate. The quickest forced checkmate in chess, besides fool's mate. And her father was no fool.

But he spotted it and blocked it. She brought out her bishop.

He brought out his.

And then...

She noticed an opportunity to gain an advantage by sacrificing her queen. It was a bold move, one she wouldn't typically consider, but the stakes were high—both on and off the board.

With a determined glint in her eyes, she maneuvered her knight across the board, revealing her queen, as if accidentally, placing it directly in the path of her father's bishop. The smooth ebony piece seemed to vibrate with anticipation as it came to rest on the square, but now the queen was poised for capture.

"Interesting choice," Jameson remarked, his eyebrows arching in surprise. "You've always been fond of your queen."

"Times change, Father," Ella replied, her voice steady despite the turmoil she felt inside. "I'm learning to adapt."

"Indeed," he said, his expression unreadable as he considered the board.

The tension in the dimly lit kitchen was palpable, as Ella and her father continued their game of chess. The ticking of the wall clock seemed to grow louder with each passing second, echoing the sound of their beating hearts.

Ella stared at the board. If he took the queen, she had checkmate with her bishops and knights. He didn't see it. Did he?

The two of them stood poised by the board, both engrossed, both distracted. Neither speaking.

But her father's move never came.

Suddenly, a thump echoed from above—a muffled, yet distinct noise that seemed to vibrate through the floorboards. It was as though an object had been dropped or knocked over, causing both Ella and Jameson to freeze mid-action, their gazes locked in silent understanding.

"Did you hear that?" Jameson asked quietly, his voice barely above a whisper. Ella nodded, her eyes narrowing as she tried to pinpoint the source of the sound. It came from the direction of the upstairs bedroom—the one she had secured earlier that evening.

"Stay here," she instructed, the authority in her voice unwavering. But her father had other plans.

"Like hell I will," he retorted, reaching into the drawer of an antique, wooden side table. He pulled out a pistol—a Colt M1911, the grip worn smooth from years of use. Its silver surface gleamed menacingly in the low light, reflecting their apprehension and determination. The weighty weapon served as a stark reminder of the danger they faced.

"Father, please," Ella implored, knowing full well that arguing would only waste precious time.

"Oh, don't worry. I'm not coming with you, dear," he said. "I'm just not staying put." And with that, her father took his weapon and turned, moving swiftly towards the garage.

She watched him leave, frowning.

Ella's fingers brushed against the cool metal of her own weapon, its black finish unblemished and as dark as the night that enveloped them. She drew it from the holster with practiced ease, the weight familiar in her hand. It was a reliable firearm—one she had used countless times before in situations like this. Her father's stubbornness may have been a liability, but at least they were both armed now.

"Fine," she said, keeping her voice low and even. She made sure her father was safe as he passed through the living room. Three guards were in the garage. He'd be safe.

So she moved towards the stairs. Ella could feel the tension, a mixture of fear and resolve. She swallowed hard, pushing down her own anxiety, and focused on the task at hand.

As she approached the stairs, Ella moved with deliberate precision, each step calculated to minimize noise. The floorboards creaked beneath her feet, but she knew which ones to avoid—she had memorized their locations over the last few hours of patrolling. She breathed slowly, in through her nose and out through her mouth, as if the steady rhythm could quiet her racing heart.

Climbing the stairs, she paused for a moment on the landing, straining to hear movement amidst the heavy silence. Nothing. Whoever was in the house had either stopped moving or was waiting. The thought sent shivers down her spine, but she steeled herself, unwilling to let fear dictate her actions.

She took the doorway into the hall that led to her father's bedroom, gun gripped tightly.

Chapter 16

The hallway of the manor safe house stretched out before Ella, dimly lit by wall fixtures that cast eerie shadows across the ornate wallpaper. The rich burgundy pattern, adorned with golden vines, served as a backdrop for antique furnishings scattered along its length. A grand mirror hung on one side, reflecting Ella's image and distorting it in the wavering light.

Ella's petite frame was almost swallowed by the darkness, her blonde hair tied back in a tight bun, not a single strand out of place. In her mind, she went through her training, steadying herself for what might come next. Her blue eyes sparkled with determination, but beneath the surface, worry gnawed at her. She held a gun in her hand, its cool metal reassuring against her skin. She let the weight of the gun ground her in the moment.

She crept forward, the old, floor creaking beneath her feet. The air was heavy with the scent of polished wood and stale cigar smoke, remnants of a time when this place was more than a temporary sanctuary. Her heart pounded in her chest, each beat echoing the urgency of her mission. She needed to find the source of the sounds—eliminate any threats to her father's safety.

As Ella approached the closed bedroom door, muffled voices seeped through the thick paneling, unintelligible but unmistakably human. Her heart raced as she listened, her grip on the gun tightening. Sweat formed at her brow, and she wiped it away with her free hand, careful not to make a sound.

Where are the guards? she thought, her mind racing with possibilities. The upstairs floor was silent, devoid of the reassuring presence of her father's skilled bodyguards. Anxiety tightened its grip on her chest, making it difficult to breathe.

She tried to quell her rising trepidation.

She knocked ever so faintly on the door. There was no response, only the continuing murmur of hushed conversation from within the room. She gritted her teeth, torn between the desire to kick down the door and the need for stealth.

"Damn it," she muttered, her thoughts turning to the missing guards once more. Their absence gnawed at her, adding to the tension that already permeated the stale air. The silence weighed heavily on her, each quiet creak of the floorboards beneath her feet sounding like a gunshot in the stillness of the night.

"Three, two, one," she counted down silently, preparing herself for whatever waited on the other side of the door. With her gun raised, she took a deep breath.

The faint rustling sound grew louder, taunting Ella from within the bedroom. A shiver ran down her spine as she tightened her grip on the gun. She knew she couldn't hesitate any longer. With a steely determination, she burst into the room, gun raised, ready to eliminate any threat.

"Freeze!" she barked, scanning the room with wary eyes. But instead of shadowy figures or masked assassins, she found nothing but emptiness and disarray. Her heart pounded in her chest, confusion mingling with the adrenaline that coursed through her veins.

"Damn it," she muttered, lowering her weapon. She took in the scene before her: a broken window, shards of glass littering the floor, and a cheap, dollar-store speaker lying amidst the bed covers, sending bursts of distorted sound into the air.

A pause, then another burst of static voices coming from the speaker.

The hushed voices she had heard earlier now seemed like a cruel deception, a mere distraction from the real danger lurking nearby.

With each passing moment, her concern for her father's safety intensified. As she gazed at the shattered glass, she felt a flicker of concern.

In a sudden flash of insight, Ella realized the broken window and speaker setup had to be a distraction. Her pulse quickened as she considered the implications. The assailant had managed to lure her away from her father's side, leaving him vulnerable to attack.

"Damn it," she hissed under her breath, her eyes darting around the hallway in search of any further clues. Nothing. She'd been tricked.

Wasting no time, Ella sprinted down the corridor, gun still raised, adrenaline coursing through her veins as she prepared herself for whatever lay ahead. As she rounded the corner, a horrific sight stopped her dead in her tracks.

At the base of the stairs, three of her father's bodyguards lay sprawled on the floor, their throats slit, blood pooling beneath them. Their sightless eyes stared blankly at the ceiling as if searching for answers to the violence that had befallen them. The air was heavy with the metallic scent of blood, and it took all of Ella's resolve not to freeze in place.

These men were skilled in combat, yet they had been taken down by someone who was even deadlier.

Ella forced herself to focus, analyzing the scene before her. Every detail mattered now. She fought to control her breathing and temper her emotions as she scanned the room, trying to piece together what had happened.

As Ella's gaze swept over the gruesome scene, she noticed a peculiar detail that only deepened the mystery. The bodyguards' shoelaces were missing, their boots hanging loose on their lifeless feet.

Same as the governor.

She knew she couldn't dwell on it for too long—her father's safety was at stake. With a nimble leap, she vaulted over the bodies, her petite frame propelled by adrenaline and determination. Her heart thundered in her chest, each beat fueling her resolve to protect her father despite their strained relationship.

"Stay focused, Ella," she whispered to herself, her breathing quickening as she sprinted towards the garage.

Her gun remained firmly in her grasp, ready for any threat that might emerge from the shadows. With every step, the tension mounted, and her instincts told her that time was running out. The knowledge that her father's life hung in the balance pushed her forward, driving her to maintain her relentless pace.

As Ella neared the garage, her thoughts raced alongside her. She couldn't shake the image of the dead bodyguards, their throats slit and shoelaces stolen. Who could have done this, and why? What kind of twisted game were they playing?

The deafening sound of gunfire suddenly pierced the air, echoing down the hallway and rattling every bone in Ella's body. The rapid staccato came from the direction of the garage, its intensity leaving no doubt that a fierce battle was unfolding.

"Shit!" she muttered, her heart leaping into her throat.

As Ella sprinted toward the source of the gunfire, her mind raced. Her father wasn't a man who inspired warmth or affection, but he was still family—and she was duty-bound to protect him.

She could feel the tension in her muscles, the heat of her blood rushing through her veins, and the cold steel of the weapon in her grip—ten feet to the garage door. Five. She careened into it.

As she rounded the doorframe, the acrid smell of gunpowder filled her nostrils and the metallic tang of blood lingered in the air. The gunfire continued to roar in her ears.

She surged into the garage, dropping to a crouch, and rapidly analyzing this newest threat.

Chapter 17

A lull in the bullets. Gunsmoke swirled.

Ella breathed heavily, her eyes adjusting to the dimly lit garage which stood as a solitary haven amidst the relentless crash of waves against the dock. Ella could smell the salt in the air, the slight tang of seaweed clinging to her nostrils. The space was cluttered with tools and equipment, scattered like forgotten memories on the floor and workbenches that lined the walls. She glanced around, searching for signs of life, her heart hammering in her chest.

The shadows cast by the flickering overhead light played tricks on her eyes.

A cop lay dead on the ground by the open door of a jeep with a shattered windshield, riddled with bullets. Behind him, she spotted a figure holding a pistol, crouched by an overturned workbench on the far side of the garage. There was a brief moment where both of their weapons twitched towards each other, but then Ella and the figure froze.

It was her father.

Ella's eyes again turned to the hundreds of fresh bullet holes pock-marking the jeep, the workbench, and seemingly every surface in the garage-turned-warzone.

But where were the bullets coming from?

She peered through the open garage door.

And then she spotted it. Fifty yards away, bobbing on the water just past the dock.

Through the dust and debris, Ella caught a glimpse of the speedboat beyond the shattered garage door. Its black hull sliced through the water with predatory grace while a masked figure manned a mounted, 50-cal machine gun, sending hot lead in a relentless barrage. The deafening gunfire and ricocheting bullets created a symphony of chaos, drowning out the sound of the waves crashing against the dock.

"Damn it!" Ella screamed, her voice barely audible over the cacophony. She ducked behind an old, standing chest toolbox as another volley of bullets tore through the garage. Her pulse pounded in her ears, her body tense and ready to spring into action. But she needed an opening—a moment of weakness she could exploit.

She raised her own gun, firing off two shots in the direction of the 50-cal, but the gun was protected by a metal shield.

It was like shooting a wall.

Her father, the dark figure crouched by the overturned bench, shot her a quick look, his eyes narrowed. His lips twisted in a snarl, and he returned his attention to the gunfight.

In that instant, a series of dull thuds echoed around her, and she realized small, silver cylinders were being launched from the boat.

It only took her a second to realize what they were as a hissing sound erupted, following the metallic clatter—the sound of smoke grenades hitting the ground. Billowing clouds of thick, acrid smoke began to fill the garage, obscuring her vision and stinging her eyes. She coughed, her lungs struggling to draw air as the noxious fumes invaded her senses.

"Cover your face! Hold your breath!" she shouted to her father, hoping he heard her amid the chaos.

Ella knew that the attackers had the advantage now. They were organized, ruthless, and worst of all, seemed to know the layout of the garage. Her heart raced, panic clawing at her resolve. Where were the other guards? The cops?

Shit. Dead? Double shit. It was just the two of them. How many aggressors? And where the hell had they gotten a military-grade, mounted machine gun?

But she couldn't afford to let fear take hold. Her father's life depended on her ability to adapt and improvise.

"Okay, okay," she whispered, her mind racing as she formulated a plan. "Need to get to the boat, close the gap."

As the smoke continued to thicken, Ella forced herself to focus on her objective. She couldn't let her emotions cloud her judgment. She needed to be like the waves crashing outside: powerful, relentless, and unstoppable.

"Here goes nothing," she thought, her chest tightening as she held her breath. With a burst of speed, she exploded from her hiding spot, her eyes fixed on the dark silhouette of the speedboat through the haze. She moved to the wall, diving for cover again as another burst of chattering gunfire tore through the swirling smoke.

"Stay down, Dad!" Ella yelled into the haze, her voice strained in an effort to be heard over the gunfire. She darted behind a stack of tires, her heart hammering in her chest. Her father's safety weighed heavily on her mind, and she couldn't help but worry about Brenner, who was on guard outside.

"Damn it," she muttered, wiping her stinging eyes with the back of her hand. The smoke clouded both her vision and her thoughts, making it difficult to concentrate. But she knew she had to stay focused if they were going to make it out of this alive.

"Got any ideas?" her father shouted from his hiding spot, his voice barely audible. He was nearly invisible now in the thick fog.

"Working on it!" she called back, scanning the area for any signs of their assailants.

That's when she saw them: dark figures moving through the smoke like ghosts, their gas masks lending them an eerie, otherworldly appearance. They wielded knives—not guns, *knives*—with the confidence of professionals, and as they navigated the cluttered garage with ease, Ella couldn't shake the feeling that they'd been here before.

"Three incoming!" she warned, ducking low behind her makeshift barricade. "Gas masks and knives!"

She watched the figures intently, her muscles coiled like springs, ready to pounce at the first opportunity. She knew she only had one chance to get this right.

"Come on, come on," she whispered to herself, her heart pounding in her ears. "Just a little closer..."

As the figures drew nearer, Ella steeled her resolve and prepared for the fight of her life.

Ella's lungs burned as she crouched in the smoke, her vision obscured by the choking haze. She could see only silhouettes of the figures moving through the garage, their knives glinting menacingly in what little light managed to penetrate the fog. Her heart raced, and she knew that she needed to act before they reached her father.

Just then, one of the silhouettes strayed a little too close, and Ella seized the opportunity. Holding her breath, she sprang from her hiding spot with a speed born of desperation, her muscles propelling her towards the shadowy figure like a coiled spring unleashed.

"Ugh!" he grunted, dodging just in time to avoid a direct hit. The blow still caught him on the shoulder, and he staggered under the impact, but he recovered quickly. He was agile, and as he lunged for her with his knife, she stumbled back, grasping at the toolbox. Ella grabbed the first thing her fingers found.

A tire iron.

The clang of metal against metal rang out through the garage, underscoring the fierce dual playing out amidst the swirling smoke.

"Give it up, girl!" the silhouette growled, his voice muffled by the gas mask.

Ella didn't bother to retort, gritting her teeth as she strained to keep up with his relentless assault. Every ounce of her being was focused on staying alive.

With a swift, brutal swing of the tire iron, she caught him square in the face, knocking the gas mask askew. The man reeled, dazed and momentarily vulnerable—and Ella didn't waste the opportunity. She wrested the mask from his face, leaving him gasping for breath in the toxic smoke.

She pulled the mask over her own face. It was difficult to breathe through the unfamiliar device, but it was better than the alternative.

Two more to go, she thought grimly, scanning the garage for any sign of her father or the remaining attackers.

Ella's heart thundered in her ears as she scanned the murky haze. The smoke obscured her vision, but she could still make out the vague shapes of the garage's scattered tools and equipment. Her breathing was labored through the gas mask, but it offered some protection against the toxic fumes.

Where were they? Ella muttered under her breath, anxiety twisting her insides like a vice.

Her attention snapped to the sound of muffled voices and shuffling behind a stack of crates. There, she saw two shadowy figures dragging someone between them—her father. And a woman with a gun stood watch, covering their retreat.

Ella began to move, quiet and quick.

But with honed instincts, the woman turned toward Ella, her eyes narrowing menacingly above the mask. Without hesitation, she fired a shot in Ella's direction.

Ella ducked behind the same workbench that had served as her father's shelter, narrowly avoiding the bullet. She felt the heat from the gunfire singe her hair. Taking a deep breath, she steeled herself and peeked around the edge of her cover.

They were dragging her father towards the boat. He was slumped—unconscious? Ella's hands trembled as she gripped her gun.

Summoning every ounce of courage she possessed, she darted from her hiding spot and sprinted towards the boat, her legs pumping furiously. Another shot rang out, followed by the whine of a ricocheting bullet. It missed her head by mere inches, sending a cold shiver down her spine.

She urged herself onward, her chest heaving as she closed the distance between herself and the boat.

She kept along the wooden barricades lining the dock, avoiding the machine gun. But the benefit of smoke cut two ways. If she couldn't see them, they couldn't see her.

She felt her fingers brush against the boat's hull, her vision blurred with tears of determination. And then, the boat roared to life and began to pull away from the dock.

Was her father on it? Where was the woman with the gun?

She'd lost track of everything in the acrid fumes swirling around them.

Ella cried out, lunging for the boat's railing. But as it slid through her fingers, she knew she'd missed her chance. In a split-second decision, she grabbed her phone and hurled it towards the boat. It landed over the railing. Again, obscured by the vestiges of smoke.

No sooner had it landed than a bullet whizzed past her ear, narrowly missing her head. Her instincts took over, and she ducked for cover behind the mooring posts.

And then the boat was moving.

Where was Brenner? Dammit.

Ella's throat constricted and her chest tightened as she eyed the re-treating boat, her father's captors disappearing into the dark waters.

She leaned back, wiping sweat from her brow, breathing in shallow puffs and inhaling the saline scent of seawater and gunpowder.

She glanced back to the manor. Other figures were now emerging from around the side of the house. Voices were calling out. She thought she glimpsed a faint plume of smoke in the distance—a distraction? Had the others been lured away, like her?

A figure was moving swiftly towards her, and her eyes stung from the smoke as she glanced up to watch his approach.

"Are you okay?" Brenner's voice called out.

She felt a surge of relief. He was alive. He was safe. "Yeah," Ella replied, standing slowly now, her legs weak. "They got him, though. He's on the boat."

A sudden gust of wind whipped at their faces. The waves churned and frothed, turning the once calm waters into a dangerous battleground.

The smoke swirled, clearing, and already, Ella's gaze was scanning the dock.

"Over there!" she shouted, pointing to a small speedboat tied to one of the piers. It was their only chance.

"Let's go!" Brenner urged, sprinting towards the boat with Ella hot on his heels.

As they neared the vessel, Ella couldn't help but feel a knot of fear forming in her stomach. She'd never piloted such a small boat in such treacherous conditions before, but she knew she had no choice. She hated the ocean. always had...

"Can you handle this?" Brenner asked as they climbed aboard, his eyes searching hers for any sign of doubt.

"Of course," Ella lied, hoping her voice didn't betray her uncertainty. "Just help me untie the ropes."

"Got it," he said, working quickly to free the boat from its moorings.

With a roar of the engine, they sped off into the stormy night, the waves tossing their small craft about like a toy in a tempest. The wind howled around them, stinging their faces with icy spray as they pursued the kidnappers' boat.

"Come on," Ella murmured through gritted teeth, fighting to keep the boat steady and on course. "We can't lose them now."

Chapter 18

Brenner gripped the wheel of the speedboat, his knuckles turning white as the engine roared beneath him. Ella sat beside him, her eyes fixed on the larger speedboat ahead, in the distance, but still visible now that they'd cleared the smoky shores. The boat ahead cut through the waves like a knife, but her eyes were fixated on the machine gun mounted menacingly on its deck. Waves crashed around them as they cut through the water. Brenner had always known how to go fast and now was no exception.

"Can't let 'em get away!" shouted Brenner over the wind. "Hold on! We're going into the breaker!"

She grimaced, her hands as white as his, though, hers were grasping the railing as sea spray speckled her face, her arms.

She felt cold, her pulse rapid.

Another wave rose up to meet them, but they crashed into the water, cutting straight through it.

But now, as they gained on the larger boat, they were noticed.

A shout, though she couldn't quite make out the words, echoed ahead of them, carrying across the open water.

The speedboat ahead fired a volley of bullets in their direction, forcing Brenner to swerve sharply to avoid being hit. The spray spattered his face, but he didn't slow down.

"Keep going!" Ella urged, her hand gripping the side of the boat as if her life depended on it.

The sky darkened as storm clouds loomed overhead, casting an ominous shadow over the tumultuous sea. Rain began to fall even faster, making it difficult to see beyond the boat's navigation lights.

"Damn it," she muttered under her breath, squinting through the rain at the larger boat.

As they continued their pursuit, the storm intensified, the wind howling around them like a wild beast. Still, Brenner steered the boat with unwavering resolve.

The clock on the boat's console read 1:30 AM, and Ella felt every second of the late hour weighing down on her. With the rising waves, the darkening skies, and the pouring rain, they'd lost sight of the boat ahead of them.

Her eyes strained against the inky blackness, seeking any trace of the kidnappers' speedboat. It was gone, like a wraith.

But she'd planned for this exact situation.

She pulled out Brenner's iPhone from his pocket and opened the Find My app. Her fingers trembled as she entered her details, but her determination was unwavering.

"Come on, come on," she whispered, her breath hot against the cold rain that stung her face. "Please let this work."

"What are you doing?" Brenner asked, his voice tense with concern.

"Tracking my phone," Ella replied, her eyes glued to the screen. "It's still on the other boat. If we can just get close enough, maybe we can figure out where they're headed."

Brenner nodded. He gripped the wheel tighter, willing the boat to cut through the waves faster.

"Okay, just tell me where to go."

"Head slightly left," Ella instructed, her eyes darting between the screen and the tumultuous ocean ahead. "We're closing in!"

As they continued their harrowing pursuit, the phone's screen flickered in the darkness, offering a faint beacon of hope amidst the chaos. The two of them clung to this lifeline, each desperately praying for a breakthrough, driven by the unyielding need to bring Ella's father back to safety.

"Turn right, Brenner! We need to close the distance!" Ella shouted over the storm's cacophony as she studied her boyfriend's iPhone. Lightning split the sky, illuminating the towering waves that surrounded them.

"Got it!" Brenner barked back, his hands white-knuckled on the wheel. He glanced at the GPS chart plotter before making the turn. The navigation system's screen glowed with an eerie intensity against the inky blackness of the night, highlighting the furrowed lines etched across Brenner's face.

"Are we getting closer?" he asked, doubt creeping into his voice as he fought to keep the boat steady.

"Almost there," Ella responded, her heart pounding in her chest like a war drum. She could feel the adrenaline coursing through her veins, propelling her forward toward a moment of truth—or tragedy.

And suddenly, as a wave dipped, like a mountain sinking into the ocean, she spotted it.

The boat was *far* closer than she'd thought. Only fifty yards ahead, no longer hidden by the walls of writhing water.

"We're getting closer!" she yelled.

But even as she shouted, something caught her words in her throat.

Suddenly, the fleeing speedboat ground to a halt, its navigation lights cutting through the darkness like a pair of malevolent eyes. Brenner and Ella exchanged baffled looks, their confusion mingling with fear.

The boat went still.

They glided towards it, cutting the distance rapidly now.

"What the hell is going on?" Brenner muttered under his breath, slowing their boat down as they approached the other vessel.

Ella's grip on her phone tightened, knuckles turning white. "I don't know, but this doesn't feel right." Her thoughts raced, conjuring up images of her father and what might be happening to him on that boat.

As the distance between the boats closed, a figure emerged from the shadows on the prow of the other speedboat. The man in the tracksuit was a looming presence, his six-foot-two muscular frame and shaved head giving him an air of menace. He waved at Brenner and Ella, a twisted grin on his face that showcased a gleaming gold tooth.

"Ahoy there!" he called out mockingly, his voice carrying over the storm. "Glad you could join the party!"

Ella squinted through the rain; she didn't recognize the man, but he carried an air of cocky confidence. Her blood turned to ice, but she refused to let fear paralyze her.

She raised her gun, pointing it at him. "Hands up," she snapped.

"Nice try, hero," the man snarled. "But it's not that simple." He reached back, pulling someone forward. The figure stumbled, cursing. The man in the tracksuit pressed a knife to Ella's father's throat, making the older man gasp in pain. "Turn back now, or I'll slice him open right here."

Ella felt a soft breath escape her lips.

The man smirked. He winked at her. "I thought so. You care for Mr. Porter, don't you?" He teased the knife against her father's neck, tracing his jugular vein with the steel tip.

"On second thought..." the man in the tracksuit tapped his knife against his teeth.

Ella's heart skipped a beat, fearing the man's next demand.

He called out, "I want you to take the keys out of the boat and toss them into the water."

"Are you kidding me?" Brenner snapped, his knuckles white against the wheel. But Ella could see the resolve in his eyes—he knew they had no choice but to comply.

"Better make it quick," the man taunted, still grinning, his gold tooth glinting. "I've got all night, but your dear old dad here might not."

With trembling hands, Ella reached for the keys of their boat, her mind racing with desperation.

"Fine," Brenner growled, snatching the keys from her hand and tossing them overboard with a loud splash. The man in the tracksuit watched with satisfaction.

"Good," he said, nodding approvingly. "Now, I want you two to stay right here while we make our escape. Sound good? Oh, also, real quick, for posterity." He raised his phone and took a quick picture of them, smiling as he did.

Then, the man simply laughed and waved as his speedboat began to pull away once more.

Ella's eyes darted to Brenner, who clenched his jaw, visibly racking his brain for a plan.

But just then, Ella spotted movement on the deck. The man in the tracksuit was rotating the machine gun, aiming towards them.

"Get down!" she screamed, diving for cover under the console and pulling Brenner down with her.

Bullets whizzed past them, shattering glass and splintering the fiberglass hull. Ella clutched her head, praying that the deafening roar of gunfire would stop. All she could think of was her father—was he okay? Was he alive?

"Stay down, Ella!" Brenner yelled over the chaos, shielding himself as best as he could.

The storm's fury mirrored Ella's own as the relentless staccato of raindrops hammered against her body. In the darkness, she could barely make out Brenner's silhouette huddled beside her. Even the wind seemed to have its own voice, a howling banshee that screamed its defiance at the heavens.

"Are you okay?" Brenner's voice strained to be heard over the cacophony of the storm and the last echoes of gunfire.

Ella nodded, unable to trust her voice. Her hands trembled as she clung to the shredded remains of their boat, her fingers numb from the cold water. She blinked away the rain, trying to focus on the receding taillights of the other speedboat. Why did it feel like the entire world was conspiring against them?

"Stay close!" Brenner shouted over the wind as he grabbed her hand. "We need to find something to hold onto!"

As if on cue, the 50-cal resumed its onslaught, shredding what little remained of their vessel. The deafening roar of bullets tearing through fiberglass combined with the thunderous crash of waves assaulting their eardrums. Ella squeezed her eyes shut, her breath hitching in fear as she braced for impact.

More bullets tore through, but now the other boat was far enough away that it couldn't aim properly.

Yet the damage was already done. Their hull was ripped to shreds. The storm was wailing around them, and water was pouring into their vessel through the giant holes punctured in the side of the boat.

Chapter 19

The icy water lapped against Ella's legs, the temperature biting through her soaked jeans. The speedboat lurched beneath them, groaning like a wounded animal. Water splashed over the sides, pooling on the deck and seeping into every crevice, coming in bouts through the perforated bullet holes.

"Damn it!" Brenner cursed, his voice tense with urgency as he cracked the plastic panel beneath the ignition, trying to revive the engine in spite of their now-lost keys. "It's no use. We're going down."

"Wh-what do we do?" she stammered, panic swirling in her chest for a moment, but she forced herself to calm, counting her breaths in her head. She had known Brenner for most of her life, and his calm demeanor always seemed unshakeable. To see him rattled sent ice-cold needles of fear down her spine.

"First, we need to keep warm," Brenner said, stripping off his jacket and wrapping it around her trembling shoulders. "Hypothermia can set in quickly in these conditions. Next, we need to find something to stay afloat once this boat goes under." His eyes darted around the rapidly sinking vessel, searching for anything that could serve as a makeshift flotation device. "Over there! Grab those life vests!"

Ella followed his gaze, spotting the bright orange life vests tangled in a heap by the helm. Wading through the freezing water, which was now up to her knees, she clutched the vests to her chest, grateful for the sense of security they provided.

"Good," Brenner nodded, securing one around his own torso before helping her into hers. "Now, we need to stay close together. We have a better chance of being spotted by rescuers if we're in a group."

"Alright," she agreed, swallowing down her fear as the water reached their thighs.

"Listen, Ella," Brenner said, looking deep into her eyes. "We'll get through this, okay? Trust me."

She nodded, forcing her own expression into one that mirrored his burgeoning confidence. He'd trained in water for years back in the military. She trusted him to see them through.

The icy seawater swirled in dark tendrils around Ella's legs, numbing her limbs as it crept higher. Brenner's steely gaze pierced through the cold mist, his voice cutting through the wind's howling lament. "We need to alert someone of our situation," he said, determination hardening his features. He dove into the cabin and emerged moments later, sopping wet, trembling but clutching a flare gun and multiple flares. The bright red of the gun contrasted sharply with the gray skies overhead. "You need to aim straight up into the air," he instructed, loading a flare into the gun with practiced ease.

Brenner then turned. The speedboat was tipping now. He lunged for the radio, which wasn't yet submerged. The battery-powered device crackled with static a testament to the boat's fading life. "Mayday,

mayday," he called out, urgency filling his words. "This is Speedboat Delta-7. We are taking on water and require immediate assistance. Our coordinates are 48 degrees, 45 minutes north; 122 degrees, 30 minutes west. Over."

He repeated the message several times, glancing at Ella between each call. She could see the worry etched onto his face.

"Alright, Ella," Brenner said after a final call. "Fire the first flare."

Ella raised the gun skyward, feeling its weight in her hands. It was now or never. She squeezed the trigger, and a brilliant red light streaked into the sky, momentarily banishing the gloom hanging over them.

"Good shot," Brenner praised, giving her a reassuring nod. "Now we wait and hope someone sees it."

The boat groaned and shuddered beneath them, icy water lapping up around them as the speedboat succumbed to the relentless sea. Ella's teeth chattered violently, her body trembling from both cold and fear as they slowly submerged, life vests keeping them afloat. Brenner gripped her arm, his touch firm yet gentle, a reminder that they were in this together as they tread water side by side.

"Stay close," he instructed, eyes scanning the surrounding debris.

Ella nodded, her breath coming out in frantic puffs of white vapor. Her fingers felt numb as she clutched onto the railing, unwilling to let go even as the boat sank lower into the freezing abyss.

"Look!" Brenner shouted, pointing to a large piece of debris bobbing nearby. He released Ella's arm and swam towards it, muscles straining against the merciless grip of the frigid water. Ella watched him struggle, her heart thundering in her chest.

"Come on, Ella!" Brenner called, his voice barely audible over the roar of the waves. With a deep breath, she pushed herself off the sunken hull, white bubbles writhing up from the depths, and followed him, her limbs heavy and uncooperative.

"Good," Brenner said as she reached him, helping her onto the makeshift raft. She cut through the water, rising onto the fiberglass and wood partition. They huddled together, desperate for warmth, their eyes locked on the horizon. The flare's red glow still streaked the sky like a comet.

"Think anyone saw it?" Ella asked, her words barely more than a whisper.

"Let's hope so," Brenner replied, his gaze never leaving the sky.

He held her, one arm wrapped over her shoulder. She leaned against him, her eyes closed.

"I let them take him," she said softly, feeling the cold setting in, her teeth chattering.

His hand tightened on her arm, perhaps to comfort her, or perhaps to keep her from slipping off.

Either way, she was grateful for his reassuring presence.

"I know," he said quietly. "It's not your fault. They tricked us. Someone set off a bomb at one of the dig sites."

"I saw the smoke. I was baited upstairs."

Brenner was also trembling, scowling as he quickly shook his head.

She tried to return his jacket to him, but he refused to accept it. Pushing her hand away, he forced the jacket closed and zipped it again. "Not gonna help much but will hopefully allow the water sealed in to create an insulated barrier around your skin."

Ella felt waves of exhaustion hit her as they were lifted by the water and dropped again as the sea around them almost seemed to be taunting them.

"I..."

"What was that?" he said, leaning in.

"I hate the ocean," she muttered.

He smirked, glancing at her, his blue eyes meeting hers from under his sodden bangs.

He glanced up at the sky where the trail of the flare could still be seen.

"Think anyone saw it?"

"We'll find out. Hopefully, they heard us on the radio.

She coughed, spitting salt from her lips, and scowling off into the distance, willing someone at the harbor to respond to their distress call.

"We're not that far from shore, are we?"

Brenner shook his head, but his look of concern only solidified her doubts about their odds of survival.

She felt Brenner's heartbeat through his shirt, leaning against him in the hope of conserving some amount of warmth.

"Brenner..." she said quietly.

"Hmm?"

"I... I don't want to ever lose you."

"I'm not going anywhere, Ella."

She smiled faintly at his words. With a growing sense of determination, she scanned the horizon once more, hoping to glimpse a flicker of light in the distance that would signal their salvation.

As the minutes stretched into an eternity, the chill of the water began to seep deeper into their bones. Ella shivered uncontrollably as she clung to Brenner, feeling the weight of exhaustion bearing down on her. Suddenly, a bright light shone in the distance, and Ella's heart leaped with hope.

"Brenner, look!" she cried, pointing excitedly at the light. Brenner's eyes widened.

And then, cutting through the night like a beacon of hope, a helicopter appeared in the distance. The chopper began to descend, hovering above them, lowering further until the roar of the blades was deafening. As it drew closer, Ella squinted, trying to make out the face behind the controls. The realization jolted her, and she gasped.

"Know her?" Ella choked out a bitter laugh.

Brenner stared too.

Priscilla Porter was glaring back at the two of them.

Ella couldn't help but feel a mixture of relief and trepidation as the helicopter drew nearer, their rescue now hanging on the actions of the one person she'd been avoiding for years.

The helicopter's rotor blades whipped through the air, buffeting Ella and Brenner with icy spray. As Priscilla hovered above them, her face set in a stony expression, Ella's chest tightened with a mix of anxiety and resentment.

"Priscilla," Ella called out, her voice barely audible over the roar of the engine and churning sea. "We need you lower!"

"Where's Dad?" Priscilla responded curtly through the helicopter's speaker system. The tension between the sisters hung thick in the air, but there was no time for old grudges or hurt feelings.

"Thinking of staying here?" Brenner asked under his breath.

"Considering it."

"Well... Me too, actually."

The two of them would've chuckled if it hadn't been so damn cold. Priscilla was already moving something, and Ella glimpsed a pulley system within the cabin of the whirly bird.

Brenner spoke in her ear so she could hear him over the sound. "When Priscilla lowers the harness, grab it and secure it around your waist. Then give me a thumbs-up, so I know you're ready."

"Are you sure?" Ella asked.

"Yeah. We're good. You go first."

As Priscilla lowered the harness toward them, Ella couldn't help but wonder what had led her sister to this moment, to rescuing the twin she'd long left behind. Was it duty? Obligation? Or something else entirely?

Probably she wanted to know what had happened to their father.

"Focus, Ella," Brenner urged, snapping her out of her thoughts.

Ella grasped the harness with hands trembling from the cold, her sister's face a mask as she watched from above. Swallowing hard, Ella secured the harness around her waist and gave Brenner the thumbs-up he'd asked for.

"Alright, Priscilla," Brenner called out. "Pull her up slowly!"

As the harness tightened around her and she began to rise, Ella clung to the cord as she rose through frigid air, her heart pounding in her ears. When she reached the helicopter's open door, Priscilla grabbed her arm with a firm grip and pulled her inside.

"Your turn," Priscilla shouted over the roar of the helicopter's rotors as she tossed the harness back down to Brenner.

"Thanks," Ella said, her voice barely audible above the din. Cilla didn't even look at her.

Brenner expertly hooked himself onto the harness and signaled to be pulled up. As he ascended, his determined gaze locked on the helicopter.

"Grab my hand!" Priscilla shouted, extending her arm down to Brenner as he neared the door.

But he avoided her outstretched palm; Brenner swung into the helicopter. The moment his feet touched the floor, he hurried to help Ella buckle into a seat and secure herself.

"Buckle up," Priscilla ordered, her tone curt but focused. "And tell me where the hell they went."

The sinking speedboat below them vanished beneath the icy waves as the helicopter climbed higher. Ella couldn't tear her eyes away from the sight.

"Coast Guard, this is Rescue Chopper Zulu-Three-Five," Priscilla barked into her headset, her fingers flying over the controls. "We have extracted two survivors from a sinking vessel. Requesting immediate medical assistance upon arrival."

"Roger that, Zulu-Three-Five," came the static-filled response. "What's their condition?"

"Both are conscious but suffering from hypothermia. We need to get them warmed up as soon as possible," Priscilla relayed, her voice a mix of urgency and control.

"Understood. Medical team will be standing by."

Ella shivered violently in her seat, her teeth chattering uncontrollably. She glanced at Brenner, who was equally drenched and shivering, and knew they needed to stay focused on their survival. The ordeal wasn't over yet—but together, they had made it through the worst of it.

As the helicopter sped toward shore, Ella held onto that thought like a lifeline.

The helicopter blades roared above them, casting a rhythmic shadow over Ella's pale face as she clung to Brenner's hand. Her heart pounded against her ribcage—the adrenaline still coursing through her veins—but it was no longer fueled by fear. Instead, an overwhelming sense of relief washed over her, settling into the very marrow of her bones.

"Priscilla," Brenner called out, his voice raw from the cold and exertion, "Thank you."

"Go to hell," Priscilla replied, her tone clipped. "Where's Dad?" She looked back at them, eyes blazing.

"Coordinates are on my phone," Brenner said. "I logged before we sunk, but the phone is waterlogged. Gonna have to access it back at the station."

He rattled this all off, his tone cool and professional.

Priscilla frowned but nodded once, returning her attention to the controls as she sped away from the sunken vessel.

As the helicopter touched down on the helipad, they were met by a team of medical professionals who rushed to their aid. Ella and Brenner were carefully extracted from the chopper, wrapped in thermal blankets, and whisked away to the waiting ambulance.

Chapter 20

The hospital room was a sterile environment, cold and clinical. Ella, lying on her bed, attempted to focus on the rhythmic beeping of the heart monitor beside her but found it difficult—her legs were wrapped in a thermal blanket, and she could feel every throb of heat with each passing minute. A good sign. Her nerves were working. She stared at the ceiling, restless and anxious. She could still picture her father, the knife pressed to his neck as he was whisked away by the boat.

Other memories came swirling back. Childhood memories. Her father had always been ambitious and had always put work above his family... She couldn't say they'd ever been particularly close. Not really.

But he was... familiar.

And now he was in mortal danger, and she was lying in a hospital bed.

But it didn't matter. Brenner's phone was still drying—and it would take some time before they could retrieve the GPS data from it.

But even this lead, in her opinion, was a futile one. The speedboat would be long gone.

Brenner, occupying the bed next to hers, seemed more resigned to his recovery. He was wrapped in two blankets. He would occasionally glance over at Ella, concern etched onto his face as he observed her fidgeting and the incessant tapping of her fingers against the bedsheet.

"Hey, you two!" a cheerful voice called out, bringing with it an unexpected burst of energy. The door swung open to reveal Maddie, Ella's cousin and a teenage girl with bright blonde hair that matched her pale complexion. Her eyes sparkled with mischief, and a wide grin spread across her face, revealing a row of perfectly aligned teeth. Maddie's arrival was like a sudden gust of wind, blowing away the stale atmosphere that hung heavy in the room.

"Chief Baker told me. Thought I'd come cheer you up," Maddie declared, skipping towards Ella's bedside. "I heard you guys had quite the adventure."

Ella couldn't help but crack the tiniest of smiles. Maddie had always been a breath of fresh air, her bubbly personality infectious to everyone around her. One could never stay gloomy for too long in her presence, and Ella found herself grateful for the distraction she provided.

"Thanks, Maddie," Ella replied, her voice hoarse from disuse. "We're glad to have some company."

"Always happy to help," Maddie beamed, plopping herself down onto a chair beside the bed. "Now, tell me everything!"

Ella shared a look with Brenner. "What have you heard?"

"Nothing, really. Baker just said you two fell in the sea." She glanced quizzically between them. "Are you alright? The nurse said you were fine."

Her face suddenly clouded with worry.

"We're fine," Ella cut in quickly, and Maddie brightened again.

Clearly, Priscilla's husband hadn't mentioned Jameson's disappearance.

"I hear you had some frostbite of your own," Brenner said, still wrapped in those double blankets.

"Yeah," Maddie replied, smiling at the handsome Marshal. "Wanna see my missing toe?"

Brenner grinned. "Sure."

She removed her shoe and sock, propping her foot up on the edge of Ella's bed. "Check it out!"

Ella studied Maddie's foot, noticing immediately the missing middle digit.

"Lost it to frostbite running through the snow," Maddie said nonchalantly as if discussing a lost pen rather than a body part. She left out that she'd been running from a serial killer that Ella and Brenner had worked together to take down.

"I remember," Brenner said, nodding. "Must've been tough." He absentmindedly massaged his right leg.

"Kinda, yeah," Maddie admitted, her eyes losing some of their sparkle. "But, hey, at least now I have a cool battle scar, right?"

Ella nodded, not quite able to muster a smile. Ella was still thinking about her father, but Maddie, sensing her discomfort, quickly shifted gears.

"Anyway, enough about me," she said, putting her shoe back on. "Tell me about this speedboat chase. Who were you chasing?"

"Uh, yeah," Ella replied, her thoughts still lingering on her father. There was no point in worrying Maddie, was there? Not until the coordinates were pulled from Brenner's phone. So instead of answering directly, Ella said, "Just made a wrong turn, I guess." She flashed a quick smile. "I mean, I'm not sure where to start..."

"Wait!" Maddie interrupted, her face brightening. "I want to hear everything from the beginning."

Ella shrugged. "Honestly, there's not much to share. Brenner came in and fished me out."

"Oh. Like... you were boating at night?"

"...Yeah."

Maddie blinked, then rolled her eyes. "If you don't wanna tell me, you don't gotta, that's fine." She shrugged. "Either of you want something to eat? There's a vending machine downstairs."

"Got any sandwiches?"

"Er... no. Skittles?"

Brenner hid another grin. "Sure. I'd take some skittles."

"Great! Be right back." Maddie bounded out of the room with an eager skip to her step.

Like a whirlwind, one moment there, the next on the move.

Ella's gaze followed Maddie's retreating figure until she disappeared through the door. A sudden longing to get back to work surged within her. The sterile scent of the hospital filled her nostrils as she leaned back into her pillow and sighed.

"Any news on your phone?" she said, glancing at Brenner.

"Nah. Still drying. They'll pull the coordinates soon."

"Where do we even start?" she muttered to herself, her fingertips tapping a restless rhythm on the sheets.

Her mind swirled with the information she had gathered during the investigation—names, places, and clues that seemed to lead in circles rather than to any concrete conclusions. Among these details, one image kept flashing through her thoughts: the man in the tracksuit with the golden tooth, his crooked grin seared into her memory. She couldn't shake the feeling that he was somehow more important than she'd first allowed herself to realize.

"Start from the beginning," Brenner suggested from his bed, having overheard her mumbling.

Ella chewed on her bottom lip, considering his advice. "Maybe there's something I've overlooked."

"Take it slow, though," Brenner warned, concern wrinkling his brow. "We just got out of a mess, and you need to recover."

"Of course," Ella replied, the weight of exhaustion settling on her shoulders. She knew Brenner was correct; her body still ached from their ordeal. But the fire in her chest couldn't be extinguished, not when answers were still hidden behind a veil of uncertainty.

"Hey, you know that guy with the golden tooth?" Ella asked, attempting to verbalize her fixation.

Brenner frowned in thought. "Never seen him before. Who do you think he is? Just a thug? Or important?"

"Dunno," Ella said hesitantly, her mind now tracing the outline of a memory. "There's just something about him that won't leave my mind. I can't explain it."

"Trust your instincts," Brenner advised, his gaze steady on her face. Ella nodded, taking a deep breath to center herself. She knew that she had to be patient and focus on healing, but she couldn't ignore the itch under her skin, the need to dive back into the investigation. The man with the golden tooth lingered at the edge of her thoughts, an enigma waiting to be unraveled.

Ella blinked, her thoughts suddenly racing. Gold. Victims missing teeth and shoelaces. The man in the tracksuit with the golden tooth. Her heart skipped a beat as the pieces began to fall into place.

"Brenner," she said urgently, her voice barely more than a whisper, "I need your laptop."

Brenner's eyes widened with surprise. "You sure you're up for this? You're still recovering."

"Please," she implored, her gaze locked on his, "I think I'm onto something. The man with the golden tooth—maybe he's connected to the gold-mining industry. And the victims... their missing teeth... What if those were gold-capped, too?"

"Fine," Brenner relented, reaching for his backpack on the floor and pulling out his laptop. He handed it to Ella, who wasted no time opening it and pulling up her notes on the case.

Her fingers flew across the keyboard, each keystroke bringing an even greater surge of excitement.

"Find anything?" Brenner asked after a few moments, curiosity lighting up his eyes.

Ella shook her head, frustration bubbling in her chest.

"I'm checking dental records," Ella said, glancing up from the laptop's screen.

"Could try employee health insurance. See which ones cover dental. Rare in Nome."

Ella looked over, tapped her nose, and returned her attention to the computer.

"Alright," she muttered to herself, taking a deep breath as her fingers hovered over the keyboard. "Let's figure this out."

After pulling the health plan records, she began by diving into the world of gold mining, scouring online articles and discussion forums for any mention of mine bosses or owners with golden teeth. As she clicked through webpage after webpage, she mentally cataloged each piece of information, determined to leave no stone unturned.

With each search query, she refined her keywords and parameters, honing in on the most relevant results.

"Wait a minute," she murmured, leaning closer to the screen as a particular case caught her eye. "This one... It's eerily similar."

"Let me see," Brenner said, moving closer to read over her shoulder.

"Look at the details," Ella continued. "Oh, wait. Shit. Never mind. Wrong country."

"Wrong date, too," Brenner said.

She made note of the case number and then quickly switched gears, pulling up criminal databases that might help them identify their tracksuit-wearing suspect. It was a long shot, but if there were any connections between him and the mining industry or similar crimes, she was going to find them.

"Come on," she whispered, her fingers flying across the keys as she entered search term after search term. The clock ticked away, each second bringing them closer to the truth—or so she hoped.

"The thing about that guy," Brenner said quietly. "He was definitely in charge. Either of the team..."

"Or the whole operation?"

"Yeah."

She gnawed on her lip and sat up, scowling at the screen. "Maddie will be back with your Skittles soon."

"Sugar rush energy," he said. "The perfect combo."

She rolled her eyes but then shifted from the hospital bed, moving slowly towards the small table next to the bed.

Even if she had to stay up all night, she was determined to find *something*.

Chapter 21

It was late now, and Ella slumped back in her chair, the relentless hum of fluorescent lights above her head diminishing into the background. She rubbed her temples and closed her eyes for a moment, allowing herself to decompress from the stress that was slowly creeping in after hours of painstaking research. The tension in her neck eased, but she refused to let herself sink too far into relaxation.

She'd given up on government records and was now on the good ol' World Wide Web.

"Okay," she muttered under her breath, "gold teeth or gold tooth in mine bosses." Her fingers deftly navigated the keyboard as she typed variations on her search terms, delving deeper into the archives of digital records and old newspaper clippings. Ella's mind swirled with the images of grizzled miners flashing golden smiles, their molars glinting in the depths of shadowy tunnels.

"Ugh, nothing here either," she whispered to herself, her frustration mounting as another search yielded only unrelated articles about dental practices in mining towns. But she wouldn't give up; it was not in her nature.

"Maybe if I narrow down the search by excavation methods," she thought aloud, her brow furrowing with determination. Ella tapped the keys with renewed vigor, refining her search parameters to focus on areas where mines were most prevalent.

She murmured, leaning closer to the screen. As the results populated, she scanned each title, her heart pounding in her chest with anticipation.

Gold-toothed Miner Found Dead. No, that wasn't right. *Dental Health in Mining Communities.* Still not what she needed. Her finger hovered over the mouse, ready to scroll further down the list.

Ella stared at the screen, her eyes glazed over from hours of scrolling. She rubbed her temples as she tried to recall a detail from the crime scene. Something to help narrow the flood of results.

"Shoelaces," she whispered, the word suddenly surfacing in her mind like a lifeline. With renewed energy, Ella typed the keyword into the search bar and hit enter.

"Come on, come on," she muttered under her breath, willing the search results to load faster. As the page filled with articles and records, one particular entry caught her eye.

1977 Miner Suicide: A Curious Case of Shoelaces read the title. Ella clicked on the link, her heart pounding in anticipation. The digital copy of the old newspaper article loaded, revealing an aged photograph of a grim-faced mine boss.

"Gotcha," she murmured, feeling the rush of adrenaline course through her veins. Ella scanned the text, her brow furrowing as she pieced together the significance of the shoelaces.

Ella's fingers trembled as she read the faded words on the screen. "Avery McGregor, aged thirty-two, found dead in his cell under suspicious circumstances... apparent suicide..." Her heart skipped a beat. The revelation was shocking, but she couldn't afford to let emotion cloud her judgment. She scribbled down the information into her notepad with determined precision.

He'd hung himself in his cell *with his shoelaces.* Just a coincidence?

"Hey, Brenner!" Ella called out, not taking her eyes off the screen. Brenner jerked upright from where he'd been dozing, and he shuffled to her side, his normally stiff right leg even more halting from the freeze still leaving his body. He peered over her shoulder at the article.

"Whoa, what have you got there?" he asked, surprise evident in his voice.

"Avery McGregor, a mine boss with a gold tooth. He died under suspicious circumstances years ago. This case could be connected to our investigation."

"Article seems to imply someone might've bribed a guard to kill McGregor," Brenner ventured, his eyes narrowing.

Ella's fingers danced across the keyboard, her eyes scanning through an endless sea of documents. She forced herself to focus, knowing that each piece of information could potentially bring her closer to the truth. Sweat beaded on her forehead as she continued her relentless search.

"Hey, check this out," Brenner called out suddenly, breaking the silence in the room. Ella glanced at where his finger hovered, pointing at the screen.

"It's a financial record of a John McGregor," he said, scrolling through the numbers and dates displayed before them. "Seems like he's Avery McGregor's son."

"Interesting," Ella mused, her brain already whirring with the possibilities. Her heart raced as she considered the implications of this new piece of the puzzle.

"Maybe. But we need more than just a name and a relation," Brenner replied, his voice cautious yet intrigued.

"Let's find out more about this John McGregor," she said, her voice steady and determined. "I want to know everything there is to know about him."

"Alright, I'll see if I can find any other connections between the McGregors," Brenner responded, refocusing on his own research.

As Ella sifted through various articles and interviews about John McGregor, she felt a sense of urgency build within her. The stakes were higher than ever, and she knew that every minute counted. Her fingers trembled slightly as she clicked on a link to an old news article featuring a photograph of John.

Ella's heart pounded in her chest. The image loaded slowly, pixel by pixel, like a curtain lifting to reveal a face.

As the photograph revealed itself, Ella felt a cold shock run through her body. Her breath caught in her throat as she recognized something painfully familiar in his eyes—the same cold authority she'd seen on the boat.

"Is that him?" Brenner asked, picking up on the tension in her posture. He leaned over her shoulder, looking at the screen. "What's wrong?"

"It's him," she replied quickly, trying to steady her breathing. "He's the one who took Dad." A pregnant pause stretched as hot blood pounded in Ella's ears, then she burst out, "Holy shit!"

"What?"

"Look."

She pointed at the article... "He's a damn facade developer, Brenner."

"A what?"

"An *architect.* He was too young to be recorded in the investigation report in the seventies... but what if he was the one suspected of bribing a guard?"

"To kill his own father?"

"By hanging him with his shoelaces."

"Why would he do that?"

"I don't have a clue."

"Got an address for Mr. McGregor?"

"Yeah. Yeah, he lives in Seattle."

"So... what now?"

"Did your phone bring up anything?"

"GPS Coordinates were wiped. Doesn't matter. Radar and the Coast Guard are out there. No sign of that boat."

Ella tapped her fingers against the base of the keyboard. "Maybe we need to pay Mr. McGregor a visit."

"In Seattle?"

She looked up, shrugged, then reached out closing the lid of the laptop with a faint *tap*.

Chapter 22

The first rays of sunlight pierced through the airplane's window, casting a warm glow on Ella's face as she stirred awake. She could feel Brenner's heavy breathing beside her, his head resting gently against her shoulder. Both of them had succumbed to exhaustion during the flight, but now they were about to touch down in Seattle.

"Attention passengers, we are now beginning our descent into Seattle-Tacoma International Airport. Please fasten your seatbelts and return all trays and seats to their upright positions," the pilot announced over the intercom.

Ella nudged Brenner gently and he blinked away sleep, his eyes focusing on her concerned expression. "Something feels off," she muttered, scanning the other passengers who seemed oblivious to her growing unease.

"Maybe you're just tired?" Brenner suggested, but even he didn't sound convinced.

As the plane touched down and taxied towards the gate, Ella's heartbeat quickened. The moment the aircraft came to a halt, she unbuckled her seatbelt and grabbed her bag, pulling Brenner along behind her. They exited the plane and hurried down the jet bridge, both of them trying to shake off the lingering drowsiness.

As they stepped into the terminal, the sterile scent of the airport was immediately replaced by something more unnerving—the unmistakable smell of tension. All around them, there was a heavy police presence; officers in full tactical gear patrolled the halls, dogs sniffed at bags, and security personnel scrutinized every traveler with unwavering suspicion.

"Damn it. I told them to keep it low-key. If he suspects anything, they're going to kill him."

A passenger glanced over, and Ella winced apologetically, lowering her voice and saying, "Car is waiting. Hurry."

Suddenly, an officer approached Ella and Brenner, his face pale. "Agent Porter? Marshal Gunn?" he said, swallowing briefly.

"Yes?" she asked, frowning.

"Er, I'm your driver, but... you might want to see this." They stood by a tall, white pillar with a *Welcome to Seattle* banner spanning the length. They shuffled aside to allow foot traffic past as the cop thrust his phone towards Ella.

The cop pointed at the screen, where a live stream revealed a figure sitting bound to a chair.

A figure she recognized all too well. She bit her lip, holding back a gasp. Her father slumped against a wall, a deep gash on his forehead oozing blood.

"Where is he?" Ella asked frantically, her hands shaking as she tried to make sense of the video. Her father's breathing was labored, his eyes glassy with pain. Whatever had happened, he didn't have much time left.

"See anything in the background," Brenner said hurriedly.

Ella just shook her head.

Her father looked as if he were in a dark hallway of some large house...

But something was off. Ella stared at the screen. There was a faint fuzz outlining her father. "Green screen," she said, staring at the phone. "Agent, where should I drive you?" the cop asked, standing attentively to the side.

But she didn't reply.

Something was eating at her. Something that made her stomach churn. She was missing something.

She knew it, and the feeling penetrated as deep as her bones.

But what was she missing?

She swallowed faintly, tapping a foot urgently against the ground.

"The chair," she said suddenly.

"What?"

"Look at the damn chair, Brenner!"

He leaned in. "I don't..." he trailed off.

"It's frosted. I see frozen marks on it."

"That's blood."

"I don't understand..."

But Ella didn't expect him to. Her mind could capture images and pictures and hold onto them deep in her memory. Most people weren't capable of the same feat.

But she recognized the chair.

Because it was the exact same chair Governor Hunt had been killed in.

The same chair...

That was back in the Fairbanks Permafrost Tunnel.

"They're not in Seattle," she said, her pulse pounding. "They're not here."

"Where?"

"Fairbanks!" she shouted, turning on her heel, and breaking into a sprint towards the customs agent.

The cop who'd come to drive them called after her, but she waved him away.

She'd made a mistake.

The Architect was too confident. He was brazen. He had returned to the scene of his own crime...

To commit another.

It was a type of game to him.

She had to remember that. The Collective played *games* with their victims, and now, she was part of the game.

Brenner was racing after her. They needed another flight. A faster flight.

And they needed it *now*.

Chapter 23

The gentle hum of the commercial airplane's engines filled the air as Ella sat stiffly in her cramped seat, her eyes flitting back and forth between the small window and the spectacle unfolding before her on Brenner's now *dry* phone. Her father, a man once feared by many, was now being forced to read from a cue card held up by two menacing men who towered over him like vultures circling their prey. The fluorescent lights flickered overhead, casting eerie shadows across their faces on the small, pixelated screen.

Ella could feel the cold sweat forming on her brow as she bit her nails in a futile effort to quell her anxiety. She found herself fidgeting with her seatbelt, tightening and loosening it as if it were a lifeline that could save her from the turbulent emotions she was experiencing. The fear gnawing at her insides was an unfamiliar sensation; never before had she seen her father look so helpless. Desperation clawed at her chest, making it hard to breathe.

"Please," her father stammered into the cue card, his voice cracking mid-sentence. "This isn't necessary."

"Quiet!" one of the men hissed, pressing the cue card closer to her father's face, forcing him to squint at the scribbled writing.

"Shut up and read!" the other man growled, grabbing her father's chin tightly and yanking it upwards.

Ella clenched her fists, feeling the sharp sting of her nails digging into her palms. Her heart pounded wildly in her chest, urging her to do something, anything to help her father. But what could she say? What could she do? A sense of powerlessness washed over her, threatening to drown her in its depths. She glanced around the cabin, searching for some kind of sign, some form of hope that would guide her in this impossible situation.

Ella's hand darted to her pocket, searching for her phone only to find it missing. Panic threatened to bubble over as she looked around her cramped seat, the metallic edges of the overhead compartment mocking her helplessness. Her breathing grew shallow, and she could feel the weight of the air pressing in on her from all sides. Then she remembered... her phone had been thrown onto the speedboat. And then she'd lost signal, suggesting it was now at the bottom of the sea.

Another second, and she realized she was *holding* Brenner's phone.

Stupid. She was slow, now. Missing her cues.

"What are you doing?" Brenner asked.

She wished she knew.

But her fingers trembled as she dialed her father's number. She hated herself for feeling so powerless, but she couldn't let that stop her. She had to do something—anything—to help her father.

She waited, watching the screen, willing the phone to connect.

It echoed in her ear.

A warbling, shrill, frail sound that caused her ear to itch.

No one answered.

She tried again, still staring at her father's forlorn image on the screen.

And then a voice.

"Hello?" The voice sent shivers down her spine when he answered the call.

"J-John?" Ella stuttered, her voice shaky but determined. "It's Ella."

There was a brief pause at the use of his *real* name, and she pictured the man in the tracksuit. And then the Architect responded, an icy calmness in his tone. "Ella, what a surprise."

"We can work something out."

"Ah, I see you're finally taking an interest in your father's predicament," the Architect replied, his voice dripping with condescension.

"Y-yes, just tell me what you want," she said, clenching her free hand into a tight fist. "I know about you, John. I know about Avery. I know about the suicide in his prison cell..."

She wasn't sure if this was the right play, but she needed him distracted, and so the words spilled past her lips.

The Architect's voice went quiet for a moment as if he was contemplating Ella's sudden familiarity.

"Is that so?" The Architect's voice sounded curious, even impressed. "Well, we'll see how well you really do know me, shall we? Tell me more about Avery, hmm?"

Ella blinked.

"You brought him up. Normally, there's pain in recompense for that breach of etiquette." A chuckle. "But you might know Avery better than most. Your father... he's a type of Avery, isn't he?"

"I... what?"

"Oh, really? I thought you were clever, Ms. Porter."

"Agent," she retorted.

He laughed, a good-natured, barking sound. "Agent Porter, then."

As they continued speaking, Ella couldn't help but pause and think. The governor... Her father. Avery, the mine owner. And now... a faint chill crept along her back. She noticed a pattern emerging in the Architect's targets. It hit her like a bolt of lightning—all of them were powerful men with vast fortunes and, more importantly, they had been cruel to their own children. Her father, the governor... Lila Hunt, the daughter of the governor, had been hurt by her father. Ella's own father had sent a killer after her—at least, she suspected as much, though, she couldn't prove it.

"Did your father abuse you, John?" Ella said quietly.

She glanced at the digital clock on the phone. Still stalling. Still buying time. "Why don't we talk about it. In person?"

Biting down on her lip, she realized that the Architect wasn't after money or power; he was seeking retribution for the pain these men had caused their own flesh and blood. A part of her wanted to sympathize with him, but she knew it didn't excuse his actions.

"John," she whispered, barely able to contain the mixture of fear and anger boiling within her. "You're doing this because of what happened to you, aren't you?"

"Careful, Ella," he warned, his voice colder than ice. "You presume."

"No, I understand now," she insisted, her resolve solidifying. "We can discuss it. In person. I hope you're watching. He has some confessions to make."

And then, the Architect hung up.

"No—SHIT!" she yelled.

The pilot of the small plane glanced back at her, frowning. "Almost overhead," he called back.

Ella looked up, hand tense on the phone. Brenner perked at her side, and the two of them shared an uncomfortable glance.

Below, the wilderness blurred by. There was no airport near Fairbanks. And they didn't have the time to drive.

So they'd settled for something a bit more in Ella's wheelhouse.

Something she had her license in, after all.

"Ready?" she glanced at Brenner.

He stared at her, shook his head, muttering darkly, and then his gaze moved to the twin parachutes mounted on the side of the wall.

"Ready as I'll ever be," he muttered. The two of them regained their feet, stumbling a bit as the pilot gestured at them. A light blinked red above the parachutes. The egress door was still closed.

Ella swallowed hard, her palms clammy as she made her way towards the door. She had jumped out of planes before, but it had never been easy. In fact, the idea of hurtling towards the ground had always made her get pensive. But now, the stakes were higher.

She grabbed at one of the parachutes, handing it to Brenner. She then snagged her own, checking the cords, checking the main compartment.

She looked out the window at the endless expanse of wilderness below. It was a risk to jump from such a height, but she had no other choice. Brenner took the other parachute and stood beside her at the door.

"Remember, we need to get close before pulling the cord," Ella said, trying to ignore the racing beat of her heart. "We can't drift for a quarter hour—they might shoot us down."

Brenner nodded, his face serious.

Taking a deep breath, she grabbed onto the door handle and pulled it towards her. In a rush of wind and noise, the door opened, the cold air biting at her cheeks and tugging at her hair.

The two of them stood side by side, both waiting for the red blinking light above the door to change color.

Red.

Blink.

Red.

Blink.

Green. They'd reached the coordinates.

Brenner and Ella both jumped simultaneously, leaping from the plane over the location of the Permafrost Tunnel and her father's captivity.

Chapter 24

The wind whipped around her, embracing her and holding her as she plummeted. Above, briefly, she heard the drone of the plane's engine, its wings slicing through the cold night sky as it moved away from her.

As they descended, and as the wind whipped around them, Ella turned her head, pushing against the pressure of the air, and she looked across at Brenner, her eyes wide and focused, her heartbeat a wild rhythm in her chest.

Ella took a deep breath, feeling the adrenaline surge through her veins. There was no room for error—only precision and determination. Her body tensed, every muscle twitching with anticipation as she plummeted towards the ground. She'd done this so many times before but never into hostile territory.

She couldn't pull the ripcord too soon. It would be a beacon for anyone below looking up.

She still didn't know the situation at the Permafrost Tunnel.

She waited, gauging the distance between her and the ground.

Radio communications with the permafrost research station had been cut.

The two cops who'd been left to watch the crime scene hadn't responded to call-outs during Ella and Brenner's flight here.

She assumed there were hostiles below... all of them armed.

And she also assumed if she wasn't careful, her father would be killed.

She waited until the trees below were *far* too close.

And then she pulled the rip cord.

Her shoulders jolted; her body tensed, but she forced herself to relax.

Ella's hands tensed on the cords stretching past her arms as she neared the ground, her parachute billowing above her. She angled herself towards a dense copse of trees, driven by the need to avoid detection by hostiles below. As her boots made contact with the earth, she silently rolled to dissipate the force of impact and immediately moved away from her landing spot.

Pine needles scattered, and the scent of earth lingered in her nostrils as she arose.

Brenner hadn't landed nearly as gracefully, but now, like her, he was cutting the chute away and limping towards her on his bad right leg.

His gaze was narrowed, his features intense, and one hand gripping his weapon.

She felt a familiar sense of gratitude that Brenner was with her this time, armed to the teeth.

They nodded at each other, saving their breath and words.

Ella scanned the area, her keen eyes picking up on the subtle movements of foliage and wildlife. She needed to assess the situation and plan their next moves, taking into account every detail of the environment around her. In the distance, she could see the glint of moonlight reflecting off something metallic from near the entrance of the tunnel. A weapon? A vehicle?

"Stay low," Ella advised Brenner. "I think we might have company."

"Understood," he replied, equally quiet. "How do you want to handle this?"

Her mind raced as she weighed the options, the danger of being detected and the threat of gunmen driving her focus. The tension in her body mirrored the conflict in her thoughts, each potential course of action fraught with risk.

"Get closer. Identify the targets," she said quietly.

He nodded.

The two of them silently moved through the underbrush. Every step was calculated, every breath measured, as she navigated the treacherous terrain. Avoiding capture or death was paramount.

Ella's pulse thrummed in her ears, a constant reminder of the stakes. The gunmen could be anywhere, watching from hidden vantage points or lying in wait to ambush them. She couldn't afford to let her guard down for even a moment.

The bright, blue moon gleamed, unencumbered on the horizon, casting long shadows across the forest floor as Ella moved stealthily through the wilderness. Her heart raced with each snapping twig, every rustle of leaves; the gunmen could be lurking behind any tree or boulder. The mission weighed heavily on her like a layer of armor.

"See anything?" she whispered.

"No," he replied, his voice barely audible. "No sign of them yet. How about you?"

"Nothing," she said, frowning towards the gaping maw of the Permafrost Tunnel.

With each step, the underbrush seemed to grow thicker, more entangled. The terrain turned treacherous, forcing Ella to navigate a steep incline littered with loose rocks. A sudden slip could lead to injury or worse, alert the gunmen to her presence. She clenched her jaw and focused on putting one foot in front of the other, using her years of training to push past her physical limitations.

"Damn it," she muttered under her breath as a sharp thorn pierced her glove, drawing blood. The metallic scent filled her nostrils, a sobering reminder of the consequences should she fail.

As she crested the hill, a flicker of movement caught her attention. Adrenaline coursed through her veins as she dropped to the ground, her heart pounding in her chest. Through the trees, she spotted two gunmen patrolling the perimeter of their makeshift camp.

"Got a visual on two of them," she relayed to Brenner. He dropped next to her, his attentive gaze already picking out the gunmen as well.

He waited quietly, allowing her to reach a decision. The need for stealth was paramount, but so too was the urgency of their mission.

"Think, think," she urged herself, scanning the landscape. A narrow ravine snaked its way through the trees, offering a potential path to bypass the gunmen undetected. The risk of getting trapped was high, but it was a chance she had to take.

"There. See it?" she whispered.

Brenner nodded.

The two of them continued, sliding down the embankment and into the shadowy ravine.

As she inched her way along the tight passage, sweat beaded on her forehead and her muscles screamed with exertion. Her breath came in ragged gasps, but she refused to give in to fear or exhaustion.

"Stay low, stay quiet," Ella whispered, her senses sharpening as she focused on the distant sounds of the gunmen's footsteps. She and Brenner remained hidden in the chute of earth snaking through the desolate terrain.

The air was thick with the scent of damp earth and decaying leaves, the ground beneath their feet a treacherous carpet of loose stone and roots. Ella's heart raced in her chest as she crouched low behind a dense thicket, watching the gunmen move above, their shadows creeping over the edge of the gulley. Brenner hovered beside her, his breaths shallow and controlled.

"Plan B?" he whispered, his eyes locked on the guards' dark moving outlines.

Ahead, the way was blocked by two large crates.

They couldn't sneak past.

She bit her lip. Frowned. Then said, softly, "Quick and quiet. Ready?"

They shared a look. "Lethal?"

She shook her head.

Brenner shrugged.

The two of them slipped along the base of the gulley, under the shadows of the guards above.

Ella could hear them chatting now, speaking in low voices, and occasionally pausing to scan the mountains.

One was saying, "He thinks they'll come."

"You sure?"

"Positive. Why not? Says the daughter's clever."

Ella frowned, feeling a cold flicker of fear at these words. Were they expected?

She and Brenner shared a look. There was no point in waiting, though.

Too much was riding on this.

Non-lethal. She nodded to the man on the left, and Brenner tensed, ready to go right.

The two of them waited, and then Ella gave a quick nod. They moved fast, like sprinters off a starting line.

They both took two leaping strides *up* the side of the gulley. And Ella lost track of Brenner as she reached out, catching the heel of the man patrolling above her.

She yanked, hard. He tumbled with a faint yelp. She heard a similar sound next to her, suggesting Brenner was also moving.

But she was too occupied now, to watch.

The man she'd pulled fell nearly on top of her.

The two of them hit the muddy ground together, and breath whooshed from her lungs. Ella's arm snaked around the man's neck, tightening as they struggled, laying in the mud.

She choked off his air so he couldn't call for help.

The man's eyes bulged as he clawed at her arm, but Ella held on, determined. She couldn't afford for him to make a sound. Her muscles burned with exertion, her heart hammering so hard she was sure he could hear it. With a final twist, the man went limp in her grasp.

She let go of him, panting heavily as she rose to her feet, scanning the area for Brenner. He was standing a few feet away, his hand over the mouth of the other guard, who was lying motionless on the ground.

The two of them shared a quick nod and then moved as one, both pulling themselves up the embankment and facing the entrance to the tunnel where her father was being held.

Chapter 25

The cold winds of Fairbanks, Alaska, whipped snowflakes against Ella's cheeks as she and Brenner crept towards the entrance to the Permafrost Research Tunnel. Midnight had fallen, casting a ghostly pall over the landscape that seemed to stretch into infinity. Their breaths swirled in the freezing air, but there was no time to think about the bitter cold.

The icy terrain seemed unforgiving and unending, an inhospitable place for humans.

Ella clenched her fists inside her gloves, her determination fueling her courage. The snow crunched beneath their boots as they moved on, each step feeling heavier than the last, and occasionally Ella glanced back over her shoulder to where they'd left the two unconscious guards. The cold air stung her lungs, but she pushed through it, unwilling to let anything slow her down.

"Stay close," Brenner whispered, his breath visible in the frigid air. "And be ready for anything."

As they neared the entrance, the imposing structure loomed above them, a stark contrast to the surrounding wilderness. The metallic door stood out like a scar on the otherwise pristine white canvas of snow. It was a reminder of man's intrusion into nature, a testament to the lengths they would go to uncover secrets buried deep within the earth.

"Once we're inside," Brenner said, his eyes locked on the door, "we'll have to move fast and silent. There's no room for mistakes."

"Understood," Ella responded, her heart pounding in her chest. She knew the stakes were high. If she failed... Priscilla would never forgive her.

A strange thought—her father's life was on the line, but she feared her sister's reaction more than anything...

She gave a small, sad shake of her head.

As they stood before the entrance to the Permafrost Research Tunnel, a chilling sense of dread settled over them. The biting cold and vast expanse of snow around them threatened to swallow them whole, but their resolve remained unshakable.

They eased against the metal door, pushing it open slowly. It moved on greased hinges, quiet and eerie.

Ella took another step forward and then nearly stumbled over something.

She held her gasp and stared at the dark ground.

A cop.

One of the officers left behind to guard the crime scene. He lay on the ground, hands outstretched as if he were reaching for the door.

His throat was slit.

She stared down at the dead man, frozen in place for a moment.

But Brenner prodded at her back, urging her onwards.

She stepped past the dead cop, her teeth set.

The dim light from the tunnel walls cast eerie shadows as Ella and Brenner moved forward with cat-like precision. Their breaths emerged in small, controlled puffs, dissipating into the frigid air. The unmistakable scent of damp earth mingled with the sterile tang of metal, a reminder that they were now treading on forbidden grounds.

As they moved cautiously through the dark, yawning gullet of earth and ice, Ella's eyes scanned every inch of their surroundings, alert for any sign of danger.

She suddenly went still.

Brenner paused at her side, the two of them garbed in shadow. "Guards up ahead," Ella murmured, spotting two uniformed men standing by a junction in the tunnel. Their backs were turned, their attention focused on a bank of monitors.

"Divide and conquer," Brenner whispered, his hand tightening around the grip of his weapon. He glanced at Ella, and she gave a curt nod.

She drew a deep breath, steadying herself before she slipped from the cover of the shadows, her movements swift and silent. As she approached the unsuspecting guard, her thoughts zeroed in on her objective: save her father, neutralize the threat.

In a flash, Ella struck, her arm wrapping around the guard's neck, cutting off his air supply. Within seconds, he crumpled to the ground, unconscious. Meanwhile, Brenner had taken out the other guard with equal efficiency.

Brenner and her exchanged a look but no words. Together, they moved deeper into the tunnel, their senses heightened.

She heard a sudden murmur further down the hall.

Ahead, she knew, was where the governor's body had been found. Two more turns in the tunnel and they'd be staring at the crime scene.

But judging by the sound, there was an obstacle between them and where the governor had been killed.

She could still picture her own father, tied to the same chair.

The feed didn't reach the phone down here. Was he still alive?

She felt a shiver at the thought.

So many years wasted between them. So much love lost that could've flourished, like a lilac wilting in a salted garden.

She scowled, her back against the frigid wall, her shoulders scraping rough stone.

"Four more ahead, armed," Ella whispered, peering around a corner to catch a glimpse of their adversaries. "Two by the control panel, one behind the crates, and another on the catwalk."

"Same plan," Brenner replied, his eyes narrowing as he assessed their opponents. "Divide and conquer. We can't let them raise the alarm."

"Mhmm," Ella responded, her heart thumping in her chest. This was it—the moment of truth. Failure meant losing her father forever; success meant bringing him home, safe and sound.

Ella and Brenner moved like shadows, their eyes locked onto each other's as they communicated without words. The cold air hung around them, making their breath visible in the dimly lit corridor. A slight nod from Ella prompted Brenner to move forward, while she covered his back.

The pair used hand signals to coordinate. Ella motioned for Brenner to take cover behind a stack of crates, her heart pounding with adrenaline-fueled determination.

They were only a few paces from the closest two guards near the monitors. The man on the catwalk above had paused and was scratching at his face. The fourth and final guard lingered near the exit to the tunnel, peering off into the dark, a frown creasing his weathered features.

Ella took another step forward.

Brenner inched along the crates.

And then there was a curse. A loud, shrill, fearful sound that resonated in the cold.

Ella whirled around, and Brenner was also turning.

She realized her mistake.

There, on the *other* side of the crates they'd sheltered behind, was a man who'd been sitting on the ground, leaning back. Perhaps taking a nap or attempting to hide from the others while he toyed on his phone.

But now, he had spotted their shadows, looked up, and two, bright, owlish eyes stared out at them, horror etched across his features.

Five guards, all of them armed.

Only Ella and Brenner. Five against two were hardly good odds. Not to mention whoever *else* lurked in these tunnels.

But there was no time to retreat.

They'd already been spotted.

The guard behind the crates shouted again, an incoherent, almost animalistic sound of startled fear.

And the other guards all whirled around at the noise.

All hell broke loose.

Ella and Brenner darted out from behind the crates, weapons drawn. The guards were already firing, bullets ricocheting off the walls. Ella felt a shot graze her arm, and she winced, gritting her teeth against the pain.

She returned fire, her hand steady as she aimed for the guards by the monitors, who would likely be closest to any alarm. Brenner was doing the same, his movements fluid and calculated.

One guard went down, then another. But there were still three left. The one on the catwalk took shelter behind a metal rail and now aimed down at them.

He fired at Brenner, and Ella shoved her partner out of the way.

Bullets sprayed sparks off the ground.

Ella's heart raced as she took aim at the guard on the catwalk, her finger pulling the trigger. The sound of the gunshot echoed through the tunnel, and the guard fell, his body crumpling to the ground.

But there was no time for relief. The other two guards were still firing, and Ella and Brenner were forced to take cover behind the nearby stack of crates. Wood chips exploded as bullets struck the containers.

Brenner motioned for Ella to flank the guards, and she nodded, her eyes flickering with determination. They moved in unison, Brenner keeping the guards preoccupied while Ella snuck up behind them.

He fired shots over the bank of security monitors, and the guards kept low, crouched behind the metal desks.

She took a deep breath, her blood thrumming with adrenaline. She waited for Brenner to release another salvo and then moved, fast, around the opposite side of the crates, over a fallen guard, and then behind one of the remaining shooters.

Last minute, he seemed to hear her and, wide-eyed, he whirled around.

But too late.

In one swift motion, Ella took down the first guard with a chokehold, cutting off his air supply until he fell unconscious. The second guard turned, his eyes widening in shock as he saw Ella coming at him. But it was too late. A single shot rang out, and the guard fell to the ground.

Brenner stood up from his own hiding spot, gun raised, smoke rising from the barrel.

Ella exhaled, her hand shaking as she lowered her weapon. She and Brenner exchanged a look of relief, but it was short-lived. They still had to find Ella's father.

They both made a beeline to the opening in the tunnel system that led to where the governor had been killed.

Sharing a significant glance, they moved forward, further into the Permafrost Tunnel and on to the unknown.

All the while, Ella wondered where the Architect was.

She felt a cold shiver down her spine as sweat prickled her brow.

This wasn't over yet.

Not by a long shot.

Chapter 26

The smell of damp earth and gunpowder hung in the air as Ella stood in the dimly lit tunnel, her pulse pounding in her ears.

And there, standing across from her, she stared at a frigid tableau which caused her to stand motionless.

"Enough," a voice said softly. "Weapons down, if you don't mind."

Neither Brenner nor Ella complied.

Instead, they both gripped their weapons, staring towards the two figures in the dark.

A familiar situation, this.

The same one they'd faced back with the boat as they'd chased him across choppy waters.

Her father was in the chair, breathing in shallow puffs but still breathing. This gave Ella some hope.

But the man behind him had a cruel, hooked knife pressed up and under her father's chin.

A thin trickle of blood poured down his neck like rivulets of stream water.

Her father swallowed but tried not to move his neck muscles as he did.

He was tense—more tense than she'd ever seen him, and there was fear in his familiar eyes.

The man who commanded fear in the heart of his employees and family looked like a far more humble version of himself, though, it was an unwilling humility.

The man in the tracksuit smiled, and she realized how his features didn't quite move. As if his skin wouldn't respond to the muscles under the surface.

But his eyes fixated on her, watching her closely, a malevolent gleam to his gaze where he stood in the dark tunnel, his feet pressed to ground still stained in old blood and new crimson droplets.

Her heart felt like it was on the verge of breaking through her ribcage as she aimed her pistol at the Architect, a man whose face was a mask.

"Ah, Miss Porter," the Architect said, his voice dripping with confidence as he regarded her from across the room. "I must say, I'm impressed you made it this far." His eyes were cold and calculating as if he were studying an intricate blueprint. The corner of his mouth twitched into a slight smile, but there was no warmth behind it.

Ella's hand remained steady as she maintained her grip on the weapon, her knuckles turning white. She had no clear shot though, not with her father firmly in the way.

"Drop the gun, Ella," the Architect continued, his tone matter-of-fact. "You know as well as I do that neither of us can truly win in this situation."

Ella clenched her jaw, her eyes flicking between the Architect and her father. He was right; she couldn't risk making a mistake, not when her father's life hung in the balance. With a resigned sigh, she slowly lowered her weapon, feeling the weight of her vulnerability settle upon her shoulders.

"Good girl," the Architect said, his voice dripping with disdain. "Now we can talk."

The tunnel's dim light danced over the beads of sweat that gathered on Ella's forehead, highlighting the tension in her face.

"Ah, Mr. Gunn," the Architect said, his lips curling into a sinister smile. "I don't mean to neglect you, sir. Lower your weapon as well. Please."

Ella glanced at Brenner, taking in the grim determination etched into his features. He looked tensely at her, glancing at her lowered gun, then back at the Architect once more.

"Careful, Brenner," she warned, her voice shaking.

"Indeed," the Architect chimed in, his eyes glittering with dark amusement. "You two make such a fascinating pair." His gaze shifted between them, drinking in their expressions like a connoisseur sampling fine wine. "Together, you've managed to track me down, but," he chuckled softly, "what will you do now?"

Brenner clenched his fist around his weapon, his breathing heavy. He was clearly weighing his options, calculating how best to protect Ella while also dealing with the Architect.

Ella murmured, her voice barely audible. "Just let my father go. We can reach an arrangement."

"Is that so?" The Architect's smile widened, his eyes narrowing as he studied Ella's face for any hint of deception.

"Drop your knife," Brenner said. His own gun was still raised.

The Architect's eyes seemed to bore into Brenner like a predator sizing up its prey. "You know, Mr. Gunn," he began, his voice smooth and confident, "I've done my research on you. Quite the impressive military career you had before it was ruined by... unfortunate circumstances."

Brenner visibly tensed, his muscles quivering beneath his bloodied shirt. He tried to maintain a stoic expression, but the mention of his past had clearly rattled him.

"Ah, yes," the Architect continued, relishing Brenner's discomfort. "The failed mission in Kandahar. Your entire squad wiped out, save for yourself. A tragedy, really. And then there were those whispers of drinking, incompetence... such a heavy burden for one man to bear."

The words hit Brenner like physical blows, and his eyes flashed with a mixture of grief and rage. He clenched his fist even tighter, knuckles turning white from the pressure.

"Stop it," Ella whispered, her heart aching for Brenner as she watched him struggle to contain his emotions. She knew how much he'd suffered, how hard he'd fought to rebuild his life after so many devastating losses.

"Does it hurt, Brenner?" the Architect asked mockingly, still peering over Jameson's head. "To be reminded of your failure? To know that you couldn't save your brothers-in-arms? And... what about your child?" A leer.

"Shut up!" Brenner roared, taking a step forward, his face contorted with anger, and for a moment, Ella feared he might do something rash.

"Ah, there it is," the Architect cooed, his eyes gleaming with cruel satisfaction. "The wounded animal bares its teeth. But it won't change anything, will it? You can't rewrite the past, no matter how much you may wish to."

Ella could see the internal battle raging within Brenner, his desire to lash out at the Architect warring with his need to protect her and her father. And as much as she wanted to shield him from the Architect's cruel taunts, she knew that any attempt to intervene would only serve to worsen their predicament.

The Architect's cold smile softened, almost as if sensing the emotional turmoil within Brenner and Ella. "You know, it's quite a shame really," he began, his voice taking on a melancholic tone. "Both of you, brought together by tragedy, bound by a common goal. Your fathers... I know about them. About both of them."

They stood staring at each other, breathing in the cold, dark tunnel.

Seizing on the opportunity, Ella cut in. "And I know about your father," she said softly. "A miner, yes? Abusive, too. Is that why you killed him?"

He blinked, glancing at her. For a moment, it looked as if he'd been slapped. But his expression, so clearly created by a surgeon's scalpel, barely moved.

"You hired someone to do it, didn't you?" she murmured. "That must've been hard. To kill your own father—no matter how awful he was."

Her gaze lingered on Jameson, the Porter family's terrible patriarch, but then moved back to the Architect.

"It wasn't hard at all," he said, matter-of-factly. "It needed doing, so I had it done." He shrugged. "In a way, don't you see how I'm doing you a favor, Ms. Porter? I would've done the same for you, Mr. Gunn, had I known about your own father's proclivities. But... my targets tend to be a bit more... imposing figures." He flashed a crocodile smile.

Ella had the sense that he was holding something back. That he was playing a game of cards but keeping those cards tight to the vest. But these were distracted thoughts given their current situation.

Ella looked into the Architect's eyes, trying to discern what he was aiming for with these words.

But he was tapping the knife under her father's chin. Jameson Porter just swallowed, his Adam's apple bobbing against the sharp blade.

"Why don't you apologize, Mr. Porter?"

"John!" Ella cut in, trying to regain his attention. "That is your name, isn't it? John McGregor? Your father was Avery McGregor."

"I am impressed. Truly. You and I could do a lot together."

"I know what you do," she said firmly. "I know about the Collective."

"My, my, you have been a busy bee. And what do you know?"

"I know you kill for fun. I know that your acolytes do the same and you keep score. As if it's a sick, twisted game."

"Ah. I see. But it is a game, isn't it? And we're both playing. All that remains to see is who wins. But it isn't zero-sum. We could both win, couldn't we?" He studied her. "This man... this... this man of influence," he said with a faint sneer, though again, his lips barely moved, "He has no remorse for how he treated you, Ms. Porter. Don't you see that? Look at him; has he ever apologized? Hmm?"

The Architect was standing in the shadows, wearing that tracksuit, but his voice resonated like an actor reading from a teleprompter.

He spoke quickly, his words finding steady purchase. "They deserve it, don't they? Governor Hunt was another. Wasn't he? You knew what he did to his daughter. I know you knew, Ella."

"Agent Porter," she said, her voice cold. "And when you tried to kill me? Brenner? Was that justified in your mind too?"

"A necessary casualty. We're doing something important here. You can't even begin to understand." Here he let out a long, gusting sigh, shaking his head sadly. "So why don't you leave, hmm? Let me finish this. You and your boyfriend there can go anywhere you want. You don't have to tell a soul."

He gave her a long smile. The shadows of his features were cast in dark streaks, like ink across his visage; the fluorescent floor lights that illuminated the crime scene made the area seem macabre as if he were an actor on stage in some melodramatic play.

But the blood stains from the governor were all too real. And the knife to her father's throat was equally so.

Why here?

Why in the Permafrost Tunnel of all places?

Just an eerie backdrop for a grisly crime? Or something she was missing...

She frowned at the figure with the knife, trying to discern the nature of the man she stared at.

"Why don't you let him go, and we can give you a head start," she said quietly. "You can leave. Anywhere you want."

"Ah, but I am exactly where I want to be, Ms. Porter. Now, I really must insist. Lower your weapons."

Brenner still kept his gun raised, though, frowning. "Not a chance," he muttered, gun still aimed at John.

Mr. McGregor raised an eyebrow, though, it seemed to stretch his plastic-featured face in more ways than one.

"Oh? You'd test me? Maybe I don't cut his throat. Maybe I take an ear..." He raised the knife swiftly, and Jameson yelped.

It was a pitiable sound like a cry from a small animal.

And to hear it uttered from her father's lips made Ella's stomach crawl.

"Just let him go!" she snapped. "Brenner, it's fine. Lower the gun. I'm safe. We're safe."

But Brenner remained between her and the man with the knife, keeping his aim steady.

"Can't do that," he said simply.

"Why not?"

"Bastard has a gun behind your father's hip. He's hiding it. The moment I lower mine, he's going to raise his."

Ella hadn't noticed a gun in the excitement. But now that she looked, she realized the Architect had been concealing his hand.

John McGregor chuckled. He nodded in appreciation. "You sure I can't offer you a job, Mr. Gunn? I have a lot of uses for a man of your talents."

Brenner just shook his head. "Why don't you lower your weapon," he replied. "We can talk this out. Like adults."

"Adults. Hmm... Okay. Let's talk."

And suddenly, McGregor raised his hidden gun.

He didn't fire at Ella or Brenner, though. Instead, he aimed towards the generator powering the floor lights around them.

He squeezed off four shots in rapid succession.

Ella was already ducking. Brenner cried out a warning to her.

But then the generator exploded with sparks, and the lights all went out, leaving them in the pitch-black tunnel.

Chapter 27

Ella's heart was pounding in her chest as the darkness enveloped them. She could hear Brenner breathing heavily beside her and her father's sharp gasp. She had no idea where McGregor was now, whether he was still holding the knife to her father's throat or if he had fled in the chaos.

Or if her father was now bleeding out on the floor.

If she called out, she feared the Architect would hear them and... react poorly.

She reached out in the darkness to grab Brenner's hand but found only empty air.

"Brenner?" she called out, her voice barely above a whisper.

No answer.

She called out again, louder this time, but the darkness remained silent.

Panic began to rise in her chest. She couldn't stay here, blind and defenseless.

She reached for her pocket, fumbling for the phone. She had no signal, but the flashlight app might still work.

As she turned on the light, a figure lunged at her from the darkness. She nearly shouted, but held her tongue and stumbled backwards, her heart racing.

But it was Brenner, his face contorted with panic. But when he spotted her, alive and well, relief washed over his countenance.

"Come on," he said, grabbing her hand and pulling her towards the entrance of the tunnel.

But she yanked away from him, whirling to face the direction her father had been.

Except he was gone.

The chair was empty.

John was missing too.

"Where'd they go?" she whispered.

How much time had passed in that brief interval? The echo of the gunshots seemed to still resonate in her ears.

But the Architect had vanished, along with her father.

"We have to go, Ella!" Brenner said, his voice firm. "Now!"

"We can't leave. He's still got my father!"

She pulled her arm away, but he caught it again and surged forward, pointing past her. "Look!" he whispered. "See that?"

She peered along his quavering finger, and then she spotted it. C4 blinking in the dark.

A red light.

She stared at it.

"Is it..."

"Yes. Now let's go!"

"But they couldn't have gotten past us," she insisted, peering into the dark. "They must've gone that way."

She was staring in the direction she assumed her father had been taken.

Even deeper into the dark tunnel.

But then her eyes moved to the blinking red light again.

"He probably has more, Ella. He's going to blow the whole tunnel network down!" Brenner was yelling now, his voice resonate in her ear. "Now come on!"

He tried to pull sharply at her, and she said, "Alright. Alright, let's go!"

The two of them broke into a sprint, heading in the other direction.

She waited until Brenner was distracted, falling back one inch at a time. Now, she was behind him, though, he was still running fast, trying to reach the exit, and keeping his gun clenched tight in case any assailants emerged from the tunnel.

Of course, she couldn't leave her father behind.

And she couldn't allow Brenner to stay if there was an explosive device planted in the place.

So she needed him to leave.

And then she needed to return.

"Come on!" she said. "Faster!"

She inched back further, slowing. He put on an extra burst of speed, though.

And then she turned off her flashlight, casting them in darkness. They'd been on a straightaway, though, moving through the tunnel towards the exit.

"Ella?"

"Still here!" she said, gasping. "Come on. Hurry! Towards the light."

The two of them now could see the glowing light at the end of the tunnel.

She felt a pang of guilt saying it.

She had no intention of approaching the light.

In blackness, the two of them continued down the tunnel, but Ella slowed to a jog, then a walk. Then went quiet, standing alone in the dark as Brenner's shadow bobbed ahead, moving against the light.

She stared at his fleeing form, staving off the mounting shame from the trick. But she couldn't keep him here. Not if it put him in danger.

But she also couldn't leave. Not without her father. As much as he hated her... He was still her father.

It didn't make sense to her emotions, but it mattered to her mind. And it would matter to Priscilla.

If she didn't bring Jameson back, Priscilla would never forgive Ella.

And so Ella turned now, in the dark, navigating rapidly back towards where she'd lost sight of her father.

And towards the C4 strapped to the wall.

The only reason she felt as if she could move towards the C4 was because it hadn't detonated yet.

If he'd wanted to cause an explosion, he would've... or he was waiting until he'd managed to escape the tunnels.

Whatever the case, she pushed fear aside, only raising her phone's flashlight again once she reached the room where the governor's body had been found. Her father was still missing.

No sign of the Architect.

But she moved further into the dark, racing away from the blinking red C4 charge attached to the wall.

As she explored the tunnel, Ella felt as if she was moving through a maze. She had no idea where her father could be. But as she stumbled through the darkness, she heard something.

A muffled scream.

Her heart leaped in her chest. She raced towards the sound, her phone light bouncing around her in the darkness.

She could see a figure ahead of her, slumped against the wall.

It was her father.

She ran towards him, her heart pounding in her chest.

"Dad!" she cried out, as she dropped to her knees beside him.

His face was pale, and he was sweating profusely. His hands were tied behind his back, and he had a deep gash on his forehead. She could see the blood trickling down his face.

She quickly untied his hands, and he slumped against her, gasping for air. "Are you okay?"

He nodded weakly. "We need to get out of here," he said.

She helped him to his feet, studying his face. "I... where is he?" she said. She glanced around, frowning.

And then she spotted something like guilt in her father's eyes.

"Ella, I'm sorry," he muttered. "It... you have to understand."

She took a second, frowning... and then she realized. He'd screamed to draw her to him. He'd been willing bait.

And she'd just sprinted into a trap.

She began to turn but too slow. A cold, metal knife pressed against her throat from behind.

It was as if time slowed.

Her mind was moving fast, and her hand moving even faster. Something in her father's gaze, in that look... like a wolf eyeing a sheep—albeit an injured, and bound wolf—had given her a split-second warning.

It was a strange thought to realize that her familiarity with her father's complete coldness towards her had left her on her guard.

Awareness of how little her father cared for her cut deep but not nearly as deeply as the knife would've.

In a way, his cold heart—communicated in that flinch of his eyes—saved her life.

She hadn't turned in time, but as the knife began to draw across her neck, biting in, intent on slitting her throat, she grabbed the wrist.

Then, with her other hand, she grabbed the blade itself. Most people think grabbing a knife blade will result in a cut, and for the untrained professional, perhaps this was true.

But in Ella's case, grabbing the blade allowed her to stop its motion. Grabbing the wrist prevented a short, jerking motion, which spared her hand from being cut open.

The knife bit into her palm, but without the side-to-side sawing motion it didn't slice.

Still, she felt a lance of pain as she twisted with both hands.

The move was executed with perfection. She doubted even Brenner could've done much better.

For ninety-nine percent of the human population, it would've been enough to disarm her assailant.

But John McGregor, it seemed, was made of different stuff.

He reacted to her disarming attack by twisting his own wrist. He followed her motion, neutralizing it. He was forced to lift his knife from her throat but was able to keep hold of his weapon.

She pirouetted with the twisting motion, distancing herself.

But John followed up his first attack with a slicing motion. The knife barely grazed her cheek.

Her father had betrayed her. Intentionally.

But this thought was swallowed by the realization that if she didn't move fast, she would die.

She tried to raise her gun.

Fired a shot, but he knocked the weapon down just in time.

Still, this spared her a laceration on the wrist, as he was forced to contend with her weapon.

But he didn't back off.

Clearly, John was the sort of fighter who, once decided on a course of action, pursued it relentlessly.

He kept coming, fast, a snarl twisting his lips, his face a mask of rage.

"He sold you out!" John screamed at her. "Your own father. He was willing to draw you to me! Don't you see? They all have to die!"

He sliced at her again, and she stumbled back, tripping over her own feet.

He leapt on this opportunity, knife raised, plunging it towards her. He pinned her to the floor with a knee to her stomach.

Breath left her lungs, and she gasped as the knife drove towards her neck.

She caught his wrist with barely inches to spare.

"He betrayed you," John hissed, rage in his eyes. "Why can't you sheep see it? Hmm? Don't you understand what I'm trying to do?"

She didn't have the breath to reply; she was too busy hanging onto his wrist for dear life as he continued to force the knife down... down... it grazed her neck, tickling her throat.

And then there was a sudden clatter of footsteps. A shout.

A gunshot.

John reacted before this last sound. With nearly inhuman instincts, he flung himself back as Marshal Brenner Gunn came thundering forward, gun in hand.

The bullets missed the man, but by firing, he'd bought Ella precious time.

She scrambled to her feet, her gun raising as well.

Brenner reached her side in an instant. The two of them pointed their weapons at John McGregor.

He smirked once then flung his knife as he threw himself sideways.

Ella cried out in warning.

But the knife wasn't meant for her.

Instead, she watched in stunned horror as it buried itself, up to the hilt, in her father's throat.

He gasped, gurgling, blood pouring down his throat. His eyes blinked as if he couldn't quite see. He stumbled against the permafrost wall, leaving a streak of blood.

And then, as Ella aimed to shoot, John pressed a button on his phone.

A loud beep from the C4 behind them.

And then a calamitous explosion rocked the Permafrost Tunnel.

Chapter 28

Ella's ears rang with the deafening sound of the explosion as she stumbled backward. The force of the blast threw her against the wall, and she felt a sharp pain in her shoulder. She looked down to see blood trickling down her arm.

Brenner was already on his feet, shouting something she couldn't hear. She looked around, disoriented. The cave had rearranged itself. Rubble fell around them. Huge chunks of ice tore from the wall, released from their confines by the explosion. One particularly large piece the size of a grand piano made a scraping sound like metal on glass and then fell.

She shouted a warning, and Brenner flung himself sideways, avoiding the falling ice.

It hit the ground with a loud crash!

Her father's body was nowhere to be seen, and she tumbled toward Brenner, her head spinning. More debris tumbled around her.

The tunnel was coming apart at the seams.

"We have to go!" Brenner shouted.

"Where is he?" she yelled.

But there was no sign of John. She thought she spotted her father's fallen form, lying motionless on the ground.

But another falling chunk of granite and ice collapsed on his body, crushing him.

She stared in horror and nearly fell to her knees, coughing as dust and debris filled her lungs. Brenner was beside her in an instant, pulling her to her feet and guiding her towards the exit.

They ran for what felt like hours, their breaths coming in ragged gasps. When they finally stopped, they were miles away from the tunnel. Brenner collapsed against a tree, his chest heaving. Ella sank to the ground beside him.

"He killed my father," she whispered.

Brenner put a hand on her shoulder. "I'm sorry, Ella," he said.

Ella shook her head, unable to process it all. She had always known her father was cold, but a part of her had hoped... here, at the end, that he would see things didn't have to be that way. She had come back for him, bled for him... Ella still suspected her father had been behind the assassin sent to kill her... and she'd repaid his cruelty with compassion... with duty.

And he sold her out to a madman.

"I'll call in backup," said Brenner, pulling out his phone. "We'll track him down."

She stared towards the tunnel. Portions of the entrance were now covered in fallen particles of ice and stone.

The ground was shaking still, and she wondered if the C4 had triggered something worse. A seismic reaction of some sort? She didn't know. But she could hear the sound of a chopper's blades in the distance. Multiple choppers.

Backup.

Ella shivered, leaning against the tree, staring in stunned silence, dry-eyed at her father's tomb.

"It's going to be okay," Brenner said at her side, holding her arm with his comforting touch. "It's all going to be okay."

She didn't reply.

How could she?

She wasn't even sure how she felt about her father's death. He'd been killed right in front of her.

Right after betraying her.

His final paternal act on this earth.

But her thoughts were moving to another horrible realization.

As she sat there in the cold and as Brenner tried to console her, she murmured, softly, "Priscilla is never going to forgive me."

"It wasn't your fault."

"She's not rational, Brenner."

"It wasn't your fault."

She just shook her head, trembling, hunched where she sat, biting her lip as if the pain might jar her to her senses.

Her father was dead. The Architect had escaped.

He'd killed the governor, had killed a prodigious gold miner...

Who was next?

And what did he want?

She sat there, listening to the sound of the approaching helicopters and shivering in the cold.

Brenner slid down the tree next to her, his knee knocking against hers. Neither of them moved, both of them sharing in the meager warmth provided by the other.

"It's going to be okay," he repeated.

Ella wanted to believe him. But all she could say was, "Priscilla is going to kill me."

Other Books by Georgia Wagner

The skeletons in her closet are twitching...

Genius chess master and FBI consultant Artemis Blythe swore she'd never return to the misty Cascade Mountains.

Her father—a notorious serial killer, responsible for the deaths of seven women—is now imprisoned, in no small part due to a clue she provided nearly fifteen years ago.

And now her father wants his vengeance.A new serial killer is hunting the wealthy and the elite in the town of Pinelake. Artemis' father claims he knows the identity of the killer, but he'll only tell daughter dearest. Against her will, she finds herself forced back to her old stomping grounds.

Once known as a child chess prodigy, now the locals only think of her as 'The Ghostkiller's' daughter.In the face of a shamed family name and a brother involved with the Seattle mob, Artemis endeavors to use her tactical genius to solve the baffling case.

Hunting a murderer who strikes without a trace, if she fails, the next skeleton in her closet will be her own.

Other Books by Georgia Wagner

A cold knife, a brutal laugh. Then the odds-defying escape.

Once a hypnotist with her own TV show, now, Sophie Quinn works as a full-time consultant for the FBI. Everything changed six years ago. She can still remember that horrible night. Slated to be the River Killer's tenth victim, she managed to slip her bindings and barely escape where so many others failed. Her sister wasn't so lucky.

And now the killer is back.

Two PHDs later, she's now a rising star at the FBI. Her photographic memory helps solve crimes, but also helps her to never forget. She saw the River Killer's tattoo. She knows what he sounds like. And now, ten years later, he's active again.

Sophie Quinn heads back home to the swamps of Louisiana, along the Mississippi River, intent on evening the score and finding the man who killed her sister. It's been six years since she's been home, though. Broken relationships and shattered dreams exist among the bayous, the rivers, the waterways and swamps of Louisiana; can Sophie find her way home again? Or will she be the River Killer's next victim to float downstream?

Want to know more?

Greenfield press is the brainchild of bestselling author Steve Higgs. He specializes in writing fast paced adventurous mystery and urban fantasy with a humorous lilt. Having made his money publishing his own work, Steve went looking for a few 'special' authors whose work he believed in.

Georgia Wagner was the first of those, but to find out more and to be the first to hear about new releases and what is coming next, you can join the Facebook group by copying the following link into your browser - www.facebook.com/GreenfieldPress.

About the Author

Georgia Wagner worked as a ghost writer for many, many years before finally taking the plunge into self-publishing. Location and character are two big factors for Georgia, and getting those right allows the story to flow seamlessly onto the page. And flow it does, because Georgia is so prolific a new term is required to describe the rate at which nerve-tingling stories find their way into print.

When not found attached to a laptop, Georgia likes spending time in local arboretums, among the trees and ponds. An avid cultivator of orchids, begonias, and all things floral, Georgia also has a strong penchant for art, paintings, and sculptures.

Printed in Great Britain
by Amazon

29568077R00134